MOTHER'S
BLESSING

BOOKS BY PENINA KEEN SPINKA

White Hare's Horses
Mother's Blessing

MOTHER'S BLESSING

Penina Keen Spinka

ATHENEUM • 1992 • NEW YORK
Maxwell Macmillan Canada
TORONTO
Maxwell Macmillan International
NEW YORK   OXFORD   SINGAPORE   SYDNEY

Copyright © 1992 by Phyllis M. Spinka

Atheneum
Macmillan Publishing Company
866 Third Avenue
New York, NY 10022

Maxwell Macmillan Canada, Inc.
1200 Eglinton Avenue East
Suite 200
Don Mills, Ontario M3C 3N1

Macmillan Publishing Company is part of the Maxwell Communication Group of Companies.

First edition

Printed in the United States of America

10 9 8 7 6 5 4 3 2 1

The text of this book is set in Garamond Book.

Book design by Patrice Fodero

LIBRARY OF CONGRESS CATALOGING-IN-PUBLICATION DATA

Spinka, Penina Keen.
  Mother's blessing / Penina Keen Spinka.—1st ed.
    p.   cm.
  Prequel to: White Hare's horses.
  Summary: Around the year 1000 an intelligent Chumash Indian girl, rejected by her father, follows the call of her spirit guide and seeks to fulfill an old seer's prophecy that she will become an important leader of her people.
  ISBN 0-689-31758-1
  1. Chumashan Indians—Juvenile fiction. [1. Chumashan Indians—Fiction. 2. Indians of North America—California—Fiction.]
  I. Title.
  PZ7.S75666Mo 1992
  [Fic]—dc20   91-31342

To my wonderful mother, Yetta Keen, and to my dear father, Jack Keen, in loving memory. At least he got to read the manuscript for this book—he liked it even better than the last one

CHAPTER 1

Everyone in the village tensed as another cry came from the birth lodge. The cry lingered for a moment, then died away to stillness. The women sighed in sympathy. This was Pretty One's first baby. The young wife was having a difficult time.

Between her contractions, the silence felt unnatural. Even the birds were being quiet.

Slowly, almost imperceptibly, the wind began to rise. Scattered clouds grew bigger and grayer, blending together and flying before the wind until their individual shadows became one. The large shadow loomed over the mountains and lightning crackled eerily.

"The time is right," the old astrologer cried. "This will be the

1

child of my dream." The powerful wot of the village smiled.

"Tell me again, Old Man," demanded the father-to-be. "Tell me what you see for the future of my son."

"He will be a great one when he grows up. His reach will be wide. He will know how to care for his people because of his travels. I foresee that he will have secret knowledge. To him will be given power beyond what was given to you and to me.

"You are a good leader to our village. You are strong and skilled in the art of hunting and war. You range far to find food for us. You bargain well in our trading sessions. But your son will travel farther, learn more, and have greater wisdom than yours. When you grow old as I have done, he will be the one to lead Sa'aqtik'oy to greater glory. Not only Sa'aqtik'oy but Wene'mu and a third, new village will be his to govern. He will dispense justice as our pacwot."

The other men in the siliyik, the ceremonial enclosure, murmured at such news. Could it really happen? Three villages under the government of one overchief?

Great raindrops splattered as they touched the dry dust of the land. Another cry came up from the birth lodge.

"Push, Pretty One," the midwife said. "I see his head. He wants to be born."

Pretty One squatted low over the soft grass that was ready to receive her newborn. She held tight to the braided fiber rope between the birth poles. She heard the chanting of the priestesses as one hears the buzzing of mosquitoes and needle flies over the marshes at Wene'mu. Another contraction started and she put her

2

mind back to the work of getting her baby born. "Soon," the midwife said again. Pretty One doubted it.

Flashes of lightning streaked and forked through the black clouds. For a long breath, the sky was light. The villagers within sight of the winter solstice pole saw its crown of feathers burst into tongues of flame only to be extinguished within moments by the downpour.

"It is a Mother's blessing," the people muttered before the roar of thunder that deafened the ear and shook the ground. As the rumbles died away, the wind softened. The villagers heard the sound of a newborn crying lustily above the rain.

"He is born! He is born!" Swordfish started to walk from the siliyik into the rain. He was already in the courtyard when Old Man ran to him and stopped him.

"Where do you think you are going?" he demanded.

"To see my son," Swordfish responded impatiently.

"Men may not go to the women's buildings." The alchuklash held him firmly. The other Antap priests waiting within called to him to come back.

"I am going to see my son." Swordfish was adamant. "Spirits don't frighten me." He sneered. His angry eyes resembled those of a hawk. He shrugged off Old Man's hands and walked purposefully down the path to the birth lodge.

The Antap men filed out of the siliyik to stand under the dripping trees. "What he does is unlucky," one of the men whispered fearfully.

"He brings disgrace upon himself for his impatience if nothing else," Old Man said solemnly.

The wind and the rain stopped and many of the people came out of their homes to look down the path to the women's houses. They saw their wot walk by imperiously and they waited curiously, wondering what he was doing.

Quite suddenly, a new cry reached the people, a cry of shock. Words of rage and anger were muffled by distance.

"Four cries," the Antap murmured. "It's a sign." The common people heard. "Four cries," they repeated. They kept repeating the phrase until it became a chant, growing in volume and power. It stopped as Swordfish came back into view. The silence that hung over the village was as ominous as storm clouds blocking out the sun.

Swordfish strode back to the siliyik, his face twisted with rage. His tall, muscular frame quivered, trying for control.

"I will not bear the humiliation," he began softly. "The disgrace is yours, Old Man, for your lies and your false prediction. I order you to leave Sa'aqtik'oy." His voice grew louder and there was a threat behind his words that was not to be mistaken.

"What happened?" Old Man asked humbly. He stood as if expecting a blow, his feet apart for balance and his eyes flickering. The villagers wondered if Swordfish would dare to strike the alchuklash.

"Your stars told you wrong. Let the Antap pick another alchuklash. You must go. I divorce my wife. The Antap can care for her because I won't. Perhaps a new wife can give me a son." He turned away.

"The boy is deformed?" Old Man asked. "He is dead? Tell us," he persisted. Swordfish whirled around.

"*He* is a girl!" The wot of Sa'aqtik'oy walked to the central keesh, his home. He entered, and pulled the skin down over the entryway of the round, reed-covered hut.

4

Old Man went into his own keesh. Within moments he emerged carrying a quiver of arrows and his bow slung over a shoulder. His bed furs were rolled and tied on his back. His flint knife was in the holder on his belt. He wore his sealskin cape over his kilt and his thick-soled tule walking sandals were on his feet.

"Good-bye, my friends," Old Man said softly, taking a last look around him at his home village.

"Where will you go?" one of the priests asked him. "Tell us," another said. "We will make sure you have meat."

"The Mother will give me what I need. If she does not, I will die; that is all."

He walked slowly to the end of the row of reed-constructed homes and down the path; soon he was out of sight.

The priests stared after him. "This is not a good day, brothers," the oldest of the remaining Antap, the village's elite few, told the rest.

"Let us return to the siliyik and pray for guidance. Perhaps our young, hotheaded leader will forget his anger and we can bring Old Man back to us."

"Don't make any wagers on that, or that he will take his wife back. We can expect trouble from her village for this," answered another priest who was standing nearby.

In the birth lodge, tears of anger poured down Pretty One's cheeks. She lay on a bed of soft rushes covered with skins. The women who were attending her did what was necessary. They washed her and the infant with soft cloths dipped into the rain storage baskets. One of the women left to bury the afterbirth far from the village, where animals would not look to seek out a newborn.

When Pretty One and the child were clean and dry, they put the tiny girl to her mother's breast.

Two Leaves, one of the priestesses, picked up a shell comb and began to straighten Pretty One's tangled hair. They covered her with sealskin blankets and built up the fire so mother and baby would be warm.

Sunflower, Two Leaves's oldest daughter, arrived from the village breathless, entered the hut, and turned to her mother. "Old Man has been exiled. He is gone from the village."

Angry shouts and head shakings followed her announcement. "You are divorced, Pretty One," she continued, sympathy coloring her voice and making it tremble. "Oh, Pretty One!"

Sadness crossed the faces of all the women in the lodge. They all admired this young woman who came to their village from Wene'mu to marry their wot.

Emotion overcame the young messenger. Her eyes filled with tears. She knelt on the side of the bed and touched her cheek to that of the lovely but unhappy mother.

"What will you do? Will you go home? I will care for you if you stay. I'll make sure you'll have meat and fish and I'll grind and leach extra acorn meal for you and the little one."

"You are loved here," Two Leaves added. "You won't suffer from want, but if you wish to return to Wene'mu, we will understand."

Pretty One looked at the women around her and felt a rush of gratitude. "My brother is wot there. If I return, he will know I am disgraced and abandoned by my husband and that the Antap did not stand up for me. He will make war on Sa'aqtik'oy. Brave and good men will die because of me. I will stay with you." Smiles greeted her decision.

"What will you name the baby," asked Sunflower. "Look! She wakes up."

Pretty One held the baby up to look at her. The tiny arms moved in circles. The tiny fingers grasped Sunflower's finger when the girl reached out to touch her, but the newborn's eyes seemed to look straight into her mother's.

"A solemn child," one of the priestesses remarked. "She no longer cries, but she looks so serious."

"She is too young to know of the confusion her birth created," said one woman, but a priestess nearby hushed her. The new mother was looking over her infant.

"She is perfect," Pretty One declared.

"Then you must give thanks to Earth Mother for a healthy child and a safe delivery," Two Leaves reminded her.

"I thank you, Chupu, mother of all, for my safe delivery and my perfect daughter," Pretty One said solemnly, bowing her head toward the earth. The child on the crook of her arm turned her head to the nipple that brushed her cheek at her mother's bow and began to nurse vigorously. Pretty One covered the infant with part of the blanket and sighed.

"What is her name?" Sunflower asked again.

"May I really name her myself?" the new mother asked Two Leaves.

"The alchuklash normally gives the first name a child will be called. She may choose other names herself as she grows older, but the baby must have a name for now. There is no time to wait for the next alchuklash to be chosen. Since Swordfish divorces you, he has no say at all in this matter. You, Pretty One, may name your own child."

Pretty One thought and the women waited. At last, her eyes brightened and she smiled. "My beautiful daughter, I know your name now," she said to the baby that nestled peacefully at her side. For a little while, it was as if there were nothing in the world that might ever concern her or end this blissful communion between mother and child.

"I cried when I was giving you birth," Pretty One said. "You cried when you came into this world," she continued. "The sky cried and then your father cried. Your first name shall be Four Cries."

"That's what they said at the village too," Sunflower said with a chill. "Someone must be watching," she added, whispering. They looked toward the ground.

"Then it is a doubly significant name," Two Leaves added.

"Sunflower, help me to the doorway," Pretty One said. Two Leaves took Four Cries from her while the ten year old helped Pretty One to her feet. When she stood, Two Leaves returned the baby to her mother.

Pretty One ducked her head and walked out of the birth lodge. "Look, Four Cries. Look at the wonderful world and the Mother's blessing on this day of your birth."

Behind them, the lowering sun gave the first warmth to this wintry day. Light blazed onto the black storm clouds that were retreating to the eastern mountains. Above, extending its glowing colors from mountain to mountain, was a rainbow.

CHAPTER 2

The high meadow smelled of late spring. Fragrant flowers nodded their colorful heads in the breeze and the sun was warm on the backs of the children. They approached, carrying their small burden baskets, laughing and singing. Their small digging sticks were clenched in their hands.

Sunflower, the oldest maiden of the village still unmarried, led the group. She sent the more experienced, the six to nine year olds, to look for the familiar leaves that signified edible roots.

"Come with me," she instructed the younger group, who had not been gathering before. These were the children above toddler age, too young to be away from

9

their mothers before but old enough now. "Gather around close," Sunflower said.

The children watched as she explained how to recognize each plant. She dug up one of the mariposa lilies. "We don't eat the tops of those, only the bulbs. Who wants to dig one up next?"

Three of the children stood mute. One looked up at a red-winged blackbird that was flying over them to land on a low branch of a nearby sycamore.

"I'll do it," Four Cries said. The five year old scratched a line in front of the plant she selected. She pushed hard on her digging stick. She piled the earth from around the root neatly to one side. When the hole was deep enough, she reached in and worried the bulb from side to side until it was loose. Then she pulled with two hands. A moment later, she was sitting on the ground, the force of her pull having knocked her down, but she was holding the bulb.

"Good." Sunflower smiled at the little girl. "If a bulb is too small, we put it back to grow some more. Learn to know the top of a bulb from the bottom. You'll get them all mixed up if you stand them on their heads," she said in her teacher's voice. She winked down to her students.

"Don't forget to fill in the holes and don't take all the lilies, so more can grow here next rainy season. Later, we'll dig onions."

"I know onions," one of the little boys volunteered. "They always smell like onions."

"I don't want to dig roots; I want to hunt." Little Fish put his small fists to his hips. "I'm too important to have to dig like the women." He sat down, challenging her.

"A person is not important unless he's useful," Sun-

flower told him sternly. "You're too little to hunt yet."
The boy did not move.

"I guess you're too little to be useful, Little Fish. We'll
have to send you back to play with the babies."

"I am not a baby!" Little Fish cried. "I'm a big boy
now. My mama said so. I want to hunt like my father."

Sunflower refused to argue. She was using her digging
stick and throwing bulbs into a basket, completely ignoring the petulant little boy. The others followed her example.

"This is a tough bulb. Its root is really deep," Four
Cries said breathlessly. One of the other girls came over
to help her. She motioned the girl away. "No, I need
someone really strong; someone's who's not afraid of a
challenge. This bulb just doesn't want to come out of
the ground."

Sunflower looked at the five year old. Four Cries
almost imperceptibly shook her head. "I guess I'll just
have to leave it there. Maybe one of the men can do it."

"I'll do it." Little Fish swaggered over to the root and
took hold. It was already loosened. He stood astride the
hole and gave a good yank. It popped up and Little Fish
found himself sitting on the ground the way Four Cries
had before. "I can gather," the little boy said smugly. "It
will strengthen my arms so I can pull back the bow when
I'm bigger."

"Good," Sunflower said brightly. "I'm sure it will."
When Little Fish was looking the other way, she threw
a grateful smile to Four Cries. The girl looked down, but
the corners of her mouth curved upward just a little.

Later, when the children were spread around a patch
of onions, Four Cries found herself working side by side
with Buttercup. Both were brown all over from earth

11

and their baskets were almost filled. It was good that they were bare. It made cleaning up a simple matter of playing in the creek and rubbing afterward with dry grass.

The small onion bulbs were easier to dislodge than the mariposa bulbs had been. The girls were holding onion shoots in their mouths and chewing on them.

"Look what I can do," Four Cries said. She held the flat shoot to her mouth, pursed her lips, and blew. A high whistle came from the wind vibrating around the leaf.

"Oooo!" Buttercup exclaimed. "You're good. Little Fish sure is lucky to have you for his sister. I would've kicked him for acting like that."

"What?" said Four Cries.

"Oh!" Buttercup looked as if she were getting ready to run. "Nothing. I think I see onions over there. I'll see you later."

"Get back here." Buttercup stopped.

"What do you mean about Little Fish being my brother? He's the son of Swordfish and Green Bough. My mother told me I don't have a father and Pretty One doesn't have any children but me."

"I'm not supposed to say," Buttercup whispered. "My mama told me, I'm never supposed to tell you."

Four Cries looked at her friend and smiled.

"Who pulled you back when you almost fell off the big rock? You know you weren't supposed to be climbing it."

"You," Buttercup responded in a small voice.

"Who pulled the man root fruit away from you when you were going to taste it and you would have poisoned yourself?"

"You."

"So. You owe me. Don't you?"

Buttercup nodded. No one could see them behind the rock and the trees. No one could hear them.

"It will be our secret," Four Cries reminded her. "Whisper."

"We're not supposed to know about this," Buttercup began. "The priestesses are supposed to tell us at girls' lessons, but I know 'cause I asked and my mama told me. It takes a man and a woman to make a baby."

"No!" Four Cries said, stunned. "I didn't know. How do they do it?"

Buttercup whispered again, her eyes round with the fear of being caught talking about secret things.

"My mama and the *wot* did that?" Four Cries exclaimed. "She wouldn't. They aren't even friends. He never plays with me like your father plays with you. He couldn't be my father. Little Fish can't be my brother. You must have it all wrong."

"No." Buttercup shook her head. "No. I'm sure. My mama said Swordfish divorced your mother. That means he unmarried her because you're a girl and he wanted a boy. Don't tell that I told you. I'll get in trouble. Please," Buttercup pleaded.

Four Cries did not speak. She walked away. Buttercup started to follow her, but Four Cries turned back and said, "Leave me alone."

Buttercup's lip began to tremble. Four Cries tried to be fair. "I made you tell me. It's all right. Just go back to your digging. I won't be far."

Four Cries walked for a way. She sat behind a tree, then lay down full length with her head on her arms, crying quietly. She had a father. She really had one, but he did not want her. After a while, she made her way back to the meadow and resumed her digging.

Four Cries did not repeat what Buttercup told her. A promise was a promise, after all. Her mother had never mentioned it. Four Cries tried to figure it out, but her thoughts gave her no answers. Was her mother angry at Swordfish? Was she ashamed for having a daughter instead of a son? She never acted so. She was a good mother. She never talked about the time before her daughter was born, so the little girl decided to do the same.

In only one way did Four Cries change because of what she learned. She tried to get Swordfish's attention. She found him unusual stones and used arrows. He looked down at her little offerings without a glimmer of warmth.

"Give the arrows to the arrow makers so they can mend them. Give the stones to your mother or the priestesses."

She turned away sadly, trying to tell herself he appreciated her industry and that he would show no more warmth to another, but she knew it was not true: He doted on Little Fish.

Four Cries ran and climbed more than any of the other girls and tried to excel at everything she did. Perhaps, she told herself, a girl could be as good as a boy if she tried very hard. Perhaps, someday, her father would notice her.

One afternoon, not long after, a group of men were seen coming down the path toward the village. Four Cries was among the first to spot them from the high meadow.

14

"They're carrying burden baskets, big ones!" she told the others who couldn't see. "Sunflower, can we go to the village and see who they are and what they're bringing?"

The maiden assented. "Put everything together and fill in the holes before we go. There won't be time to come back today." She suited actions to words herself. Soon, they were finished and ready to go home.

"Aren't you going to wash first?" she asked as the girl continued without stopping at the creek with the others.

"I'll wash later," Four Cries called back. "No one's going to notice me anyway."

She ran to lay down her basket next to the storage bins. The men were in the square now and were putting their big baskets next to the siliyik in the center of the village.

Four Cries found her mother among the crowds coming to greet the men. "Who are they, Mama?" she asked.

"Men from Wene'mu," she exclaimed happily. "Seahawk!" she called. "Your uncle is here, Four Cries, and look at you!"

Four Cries noticed she was still covered with earth as the tallest man came over to them and grabbed her mother in a strong embrace.

"This must be little Four Cries," her uncle said, laughing as he swooped her up and up, ignoring how dirty she was making him. "I had to come with the traders to see how my little niece is growing up. It's time you came for a visit to Wene'mu, Four Cries. Your cousins want to meet you and teach you to swim in the ocean. I think you're big enough now."

She wrapped her arms and legs around her uncle. "I am growing up. I want a name for a bigger person. Four

15

Cries is such a baby name. Mother said I could pick another name. I'm a child now, not a baby."

"Then you'd best stand on your feet," her uncle said, setting her down gently. "Hmm. If it was up to me, I'd call you Dirty Child. How do you like that for a name?"

Four Cries thought for a moment. "Just Child. I want my name to be Child."

The villagers were going through the baskets of fish and seafood and sealskins. There were other baskets that were still covered. "We'll begin the trading soon," Seahawk said.

"Trading after food," Swordfish announced. "The stew is almost ready."

"Ah, my brother-in-law," Seahawk said.

"We will talk later," Swordfish said, turning away. "Dirty children ought to wash before food," he added loudly enough for the newly named Child to hear.

"Go wash, Child," said her mother, looking embarrassed.

Child ran to do as Pretty One bid her, but she wondered at the expression on her mother's face and the confusion on Seahawk's.

16

CHAPTER 3

By the time Child finished her washing and returned to her keesh, Uncle Seahawk and Pretty One were in the middle of a heated discussion. The girl looked from one to the other, not sure of her welcome.

"Go play outside for a while, Daughter. Your uncle and I have important things to talk over."

Child walked out and around to the back of the structure. Well, they didn't say where she must play. Here was as good a place as any. She took her colored stones out of her pouch and drew a circle in the dirt, with a cross in the center.

"Red closest to center," she said in one voice. "No, the green-tinted one," she said in another. She played against herself for pine needles, throwing the stones up and watching where they fell. She played quietly, not wanting to miss what was being said inside.

"Not one of my men knew?" It seemed to Child that Uncle was repeating himself.

"I knew they would report it to you. Swordfish has not done me any harm. The only hurt was to my pride. The people, especially the Antap, have been very kind. They don't exclude me from anything. They bring me meat. I take my turn at the grinding stones and the cooking bowls to keep busy. Two Leaves and my other friends visit me in my keesh. Her daughter, Sunflower, well I shouldn't say it, but I can see that she favors my child above the other children. She loves her like a sister."

"You're defending the village of the man who insulted you. They should have put him down and married you to the next wot."

"It's not done like that. You know they couldn't. He was within his rights even though it hurt me."

"You still want him for your husband, don't you?"

Child trembled outside and her hand caught the stones in midair before their noise could keep her from hearing her mother's answer.

"No. No. I don't want him. I'll never want a man that way again. But the people here are kind. I plead for them. Don't make war."

Child heard the tightness in her mother's throat by the way her words came out. She waited for what Seahawk would say next.

One of Seahawk's young men was just walking by and saw Child listening behind the keesh where he knew his wot was visiting with his sister.

"Gambling by yourself, eh?" he asked loudly as he walked up to her. "It looks like you need a partner." He was not going to let her listen, she realized, but he was not fooling her.

"Oh, I don't know," she responded, half a smile tugging at her lips. "I was winning."

"I'll bet you asphaltum balls against pine needles," he said, sitting down beside her. "Asphaltum is very useful. You can give it to your mother to make her baskets watertight, or you can use them to stick decorations to the rim of wooden bowls."

"I know that, but my pine needles are useful too. You can make baskets out of them and you can use them to pick your teeth."

"I'm sure you can. My name is Crab. I'll be green and you be red. Do we have a bet?" He held out his hand to her. She took it and shook it once. The voices inside became so low she could no longer hear them, but she hardly noticed. She was concentrating on beating Crab.

The seafood the traders brought was part of dinner. After dinner, the children were sent to bed. Child knew her uncle and his traders from the village near the ocean were going to go to the siliyik to trade with Swordfish and his Antap priests. She wished she could watch.

She knew the men from Wene'mu and the men from Sa'aqtik'oy were going to sit on opposite sides of the siliyik with their wares between them. The Antap men and women priests were going to put their hair into coils across the back of their heads with decorated wooden or bone hairpins, and paint zigzags or stripes on their faces. It would have been exciting to see the bargaining. Maybe she could watch someday when she got bigger.

19

Her father was on one side and her uncle was on the other. Who was going to make the best bargains? What was going to happen? She began to doze off, but her dreams became troubled. People were angry. There was something wrong.

Child heard the shouting in her bed. She sat up suddenly in the bunk above her mother's bed. "Mama!" She was frightened. She leaned over the edge to see her mother sit up as well and walk to the doorway. "Why is there shouting? Is Uncle angry at Swordfish? What's going to happen to us?" Adults were not supposed to raise their voices in anger.

"Let me listen," Pretty One said.

Child heard the heavy steps approaching first. "They're coming here!" Seahawk, Crab, and several others entered Pretty One's keesh. The men found places on the floor to spread out their sleeping furs.

"Seahawk, what's wrong?" Pretty One asked. "What is wrong?" In the glow of the small fire, Child could barely see anyone's face. The dark figures around her made quick, agitated movements, readying themselves for sleep, while Seahawk stood as still as a stone near the fire in the center of the keesh.

"We stay tonight under truce," he said. Mother drew in her breath. "There will be no more trade between Wene'mu and Sa'aqtik'oy until Swordfish apologizes for his actions and the words he said. There will be no more visits and no marriages between the villages. You leave with us in the morning. Sleep now."

It was not very late. The fire had burned to glowing embers and one of the men had covered them with sand. The moon shone in through the smoke hole when Child awoke to the sound of someone moving. She saw Crab, the young man she gambled with, rise to go out of doors. He probably has to make water, she thought. Well, I do too, so I will go and talk to him.

She lowered herself to the floor and walked as silently as she could over the sleeping bodies. Baskets were outside the entrance to her keesh. Under truce, nothing could be touched. She saw Crab walk away from the midden and she followed him as soon as she was able.

Crab stood near the fence of the cemetery, a short walk from the village. Child did not want to call out loud to him, but before she was close enough to whisper, she saw someone else running under the moonlight. From the darkness under the pines, she saw the figures of Sunflower and Crab come together and join in a quick embrace.

She walked away from the trees, into the open and toward them. A twig broke under her foot. Crab spun to the sound of the noise, holding Sunflower protectively. With his other hand, he reached for the flint knife in his belt.

"It's only me. Don't be afraid," Child whispered loudly, closing the distance between them.

"Four Cries," Sunflower almost shouted in her relief.

"My name is Child now. I just changed it today so I excuse you for not knowing. My uncle said there can be no more marriages between our villages. What are you going to do?"

"How old is this child?" Crab asked Sunflower, looking at the little girl suspiciously, as if not quite sure what to make of her.

"She has an old head for a small girl, but she has only

lived through five summers. We don't know what we're going to do, Child. Does your mama know you are out of bed?"

"She knows. She thinks I went to the midden. She's right. I did."

Sunflower smiled. "Child always does as she should. Then, she does a little more."

"We must move. Anyone can see us here," Child warned them. "Come with me." Soon, they were hidden in the shadow of the pines, away from the moonlight. The crickets were making music all around them and an owl hooted as she began an evening's hunt.

The two young adults listened as Child spoke to them. "My uncle said we are leaving in the morning. If peace is not made soon, you will not be able to marry. Why don't you wait awhile and then, if nothing changes, both of you go to Shisholop and make a home there. It's not too far away."

Sunflower hugged the little girl. "We'll work out our problems ourselves, but thank you for worrying about us.

"It's very late. You must go back to bed now. We want to talk a little longer, just the two of us. Then we'll go home too."

"Don't take too long," Child cautioned them. "Someone will notice and ask you questions."

As the small girl walked away, Crab turned to Sunflower, amazement coloring his voice. "Is she always like this?" he asked.

"It's only a game to her," she assured him. "It must be."

CHAPTER 4

Child did her best to keep up with the traders, but her legs hurt. The trail to Wene'mu was long. Seahawk walked fast, angry at having been cheated. He did not get good value for his trade items. They were perishable so he gave in, but now he did not appear to be thinking of his niece.

Pretty One coaxed the girl to allow herself to be carried, but even so, soon mother and daughter were so far behind as to be out of sight. Crab ran back every so often to see where they were, waved, and ran back to the line.

After a while, Pretty One and Child rounded a bend in the road. They saw the men sprawled out in the shade of a sycamore tree, resting and eating their midday meal.

Pretty One walked straight to her brother and set Child down on the ground before him.

"Seahawk, you insisted we leave our home and come with you. Now Child is half your responsibility. Either walk slower or carry her yourself."

Seahawk sat very still, surprise on his face, while Pretty One helped herself to food from one of the baskets and made herself comfortable. Then he broke out in a loud laugh. "Sister," he said, "you have never lost your way with words."

The men smiled at this exchange. Their wot had not lost face after all if he could laugh.

"Child," he asked, "are we walking too fast for you?"

"We were all right, Uncle. I wasn't really very tired," she lied, "but my legs aren't so long as yours and I had to run."

"Hmm. I see." He nodded approvingly. "How would you like to ride in my basket? If you don't mind smelling like a clam, I can carry you. You can swim later so you'll smell good for supper." She nodded and climbed into the basket, still eating her meat and fruit.

"I'm ready." It was wonderful, Child thought, to be higher than anyone else. She stood in the strongly woven basket, holding on to the rim and drinking in the salty air while Seahawk covered the distance quickly on his long legs. They were swiftly approaching the ocean, where the mountains drop down to the sea.

"There are the sand dunes, Child." Seahawk pointed them out to her as they came into sight. A great panoramic view lay before them. She saw the wide triangle of land that jutted into the ocean. The ocean sparkled like no body of water she had ever seen before. It moved as if it were alive. Birds flew over it, gathered their wings close, and dove in, coming back up with fish in their beaks. She could hardly wait to get closer.

Beside the windswept dunes were the marshes her mother had spoken of many times in her stories about her home village beside the sea. They were covered with tule reeds and cattails. When they were nearer, she was able to see blue needle flies hover and dart through the reeds above the still water, and mosquitoes skate on the surface.

"You can't drink this water. It's brackish. That means it would make you sick," Seahawk explained. "You can't drink the water of the ocean either. It's salty. We'll show you where to find a good stream later. In the meantime, there will be water baskets in the houses if you're thirsty."

"I know what salt is." Child was proud of possessing this information. "It's one of the things the men from Wene'mu bring to my village."

Seahawk stopped suddenly, making Child almost tumble out of the basket on his back. "Wene'mu is your village now," he said. "Remember that. There it is now."

She could see the neat rows of houses now. It looks so much like Sa'aqtik'oy, she thought, just a little sadly. The houses were the same semicircular shape and made of tule reeds. The day was growing late. Smoke curled lazily out of the smoke holes. There's the siliyak and there's the temescal, the sweathouse where people go to be purified. There's the cemetery. Mother's mother and father must be there. There is the playing field for archery and shinny. Its floor is sand instead of pressed-down grass. Oh, and there's the biggest keesh right in the center of the village. It must belong to the wot here just like the biggest house belongs to Swordfish at home.

Then she had another thought. Seahawk lives in the wot's keesh. My uncle is wot here! Will I live with him in such a big house? Do I have cousins?

"Put me down," she called loudly. "I want to be on the ground."

Uncle got down on one knee. Child climbed out of the basket and ran into the village. The dogs barked gleefully as the men approached, but first they had to inspect her. Their tails waved in friendship, so she stood still to let them smell her.

"They think I'm a big fish," she called to her uncle and her mother. She scratched them, and laughed when their tongues tickled her. Then the dogs ran to the men, tails wagging even more wildly, begging for pieces of meat.

A gang of children ran down the path, bearing down on the new girl. "Who are you?" a boy a few years older than Child asked her. The other boys and girls hung back, eyeing her. He must be their leader.

"I'm Child." Something told her not to say too much too fast. It would be best to know something more before she told him why she was there and why Seahawk had been letting her ride in his basket. "Who are you?"

"I'm Otter. Seahawk is my father. He's the wot here."

Child's eyes opened wide. "You're his son," she said loudly. "You live in the wot's keesh."

Otter nodded, pleased to have made an impression so quickly on the newcomer. "Are you visiting us? Is that woman your mother? Is my father taking another wife?"

"Oh no. He can't marry her. She's his sister. We lived in Sa'aqtik'oy. You're my cousin. Otter, I never saw the ocean before. Will you show it to me?" Child was making herself at home already.

Child learned many things during the next three years, but not everything she wished to. One morning, she was kneeling beside the tide pools with the other children, seeing what a storm had left behind. Stranded and helpless in the small pools were crabs and starfish, urchins and small lobsters. A few of the older children thought to bring baskets with them before they left the village so they could take these delicacies home to their mothers for the cooking baskets.

Child noticed her friend Squirrel ignoring this easy source of food. She had gone farther down the beach with her basket and was busy filling it with the tiny blue shells that almost covered the low beach near the surf.

"What are you doing?" Child called. Her friend motioned her to come closer. Regretfully, Child placed her pretty starfish back into the pool and joined her friend. Squirrel was a girl of ten summers; her father belonged to the Brotherhood of the Tomol and her mother was a member of the money makers.

"I'm going to make some money," Squirrel answered out of hearing of the others. "You know, if too many people start making money, it will be worth less, so only we are allowed, but I'll show you. I'll let you help me if you want."

Child agreed quickly.

"Find me some strong, skinny seaweed to string it on while I get the shells ready," Squirrel directed. Child walked along the beach, close to the line of high tide. There was a good amount of seaweed washed up. Child spied and then pulled out strands of strong brown weed, releasing it from the tangles of kelp.

"Is this the right kind?" she asked when she got back.

"It's good. I think it will work. I'm ready to start apprenticing to the money makers. You're eight now. It's time to start thinking about what you'll do when you grow up. Bring me some more."

By the time Child was back, Squirrel had a rough stone on which she worked the shape of the shells until they were uniformly round. "I'm going to bring the rest back to my mother, but first I want to show her how well I am learning."

She fished in the pockets of the net belt she had tied around her waist and pulled out a long piece of stone with a peculiar shape at its thin point. As interested as Child was in the stone her friend grasped, she also came to the conclusion that it might be useful to wear a similar belt. The older girls sometimes wore skirts of bark or fur or even plant fibers. The older boys seldom wore more than these belts.

"This is chert. It's a good stone for a tool, like flint. We usually get ours from the Michumash, the people who live on the islands. Their name really means people who make money. They have different words than we do. Long ago, they taught the shore people how to make money.

"Now watch what I do. You see how my tool is rubbed to a point?" She put one of the olivella shells on a rock and pressed her chert drill into the middle, giving it a twist. She drilled a clean hole through the center and then handed the drill to Child.

Child was able to get a hole in the shell, but it took her a few tries until she had placed it properly. Squirrel waited until she had a pile of them. Then she told her to stop.

"Now watch," she said. She made the knot very carefully, allowing Child to see how it was done. Then she began to string the shells. Several times she measured the string against her hand, wrapping it all the way around and a little more. When she was satisfied, she tied it off.

"It's money!" Child said.

"Not quite yet. We have to smooth it on sandstone." When she was done, she held out the finished product for Child to inspect.

Child was properly impressed, and soon the two girls were running back along the beach, the money string concealed in Squirrel's belt. They were halfway back to the village when they saw a group of men working over one of the large plank canoes, the boats they called tomols. "Oh," she said. "I never saw a tomol being made."

"We aren't allowed to watch. They are the Brotherhood of the Tomol. Run past them without looking." Child followed Squirrel's example and ran past, keeping her eyes looking out over the ocean.

Squirrel's mother was not pleased. "The string is good, Child," she commented, "but Squirrel should not have allowed you to watch, much less to help. You have not asked, nor have you been granted permission to join the money-making brotherhood."

Child did not know what to say. Squirrel stood embarrassed. At last Squirrel's mother took pity.

"Child, has no one ever told you that there are rules?" Child shook her head, neither ashamed nor defiant. It was simply the truth.

"No."

29

"Well then, I will tell you. Perhaps your mother thought you were too young or perhaps when she left us to live in Sa'aqtik'oy, she forgot our rules."

Child shut her mind to Squirrel's mother. This woman did not like Pretty One. Perhaps she was jealous that no wot had ever chosen her. She went on to explain about the caste system, a fact Child noticed but never ascribed any significance to.

"The lowborn," she said, "are expected to do the rough work. They can gather and dig and haul, but they may not join any of the craft guilds. The common people, well, they can be net makers and basket makers. They grind the acorns and the chia for the rest of us. They may even be hunters or traders. Only the elite may join the Antap priesthood, the fishers, the money makers, and most especially, the Brotherhood of the Tomol. Only of the elite may a wot be chosen to govern a village."

"What may I be, then?" Child had no idea into which of these categories she might fall.

"Oh, whatever you wish. Of course you may never be a tomol builder. That brotherhood is only for the men. Neither that nor a wot."

"You mean I may be a priestess?"

"Of course. After all, you are the niece of one wot and the daughter— Well, I've said enough. If you wish to be accepted into any of the craft guilds, you must ask. Do you understand?"

"Yes," Child said. Then she turned away. She had learned and was not very happy with her learning. What she wanted was to learn to do, not rules about when she could learn, and what and how.

A few nights later, very late, Child took the trail to the beach and down to the lagoon where the tomols were built. No one was there. She only wanted to feel and to know the great boats. She saw them often in the daytime, riding proudly, their hulls painted red and decorated with little shells.

Now she wanted to touch and smell the planks, worked with only stone and shell and fitted together, tied, and coated with asphaltum to make them seaworthy. She climbed inside. She felt the planks and smelled the tar and the timber. She let her mind know the great boat. Then, silently, she let herself drop down to the sand, and made her way home.

CHAPTER 5

Child learned how to get her questions answered. She politely asked one guild after another to accept her on a trial basis to see if she was suited for their work. There was more than one way to skin a rabbit, she thought, happy with herself as she tried her hand at everything.

She learned to weave mats and baskets, and to sew skins into sleeping blankets and winter capes. She learned how to make nets out of sea grass and milkweed fibers. She learned the method of tying on the wooden floats that kept the nets suspended in the water and the stone sinkers that kept them vertical.

She learned how to make fish traps of willow strip and how to chase fish into them in the freshwater creeks. She even learned something new about the soap plant: that it could, when pounded, be swished in a pond to drug the fish. They would then come floating to the surface, where they could be gathered in by hand from a small reed canoe.

In another guild, she learned to make fishhooks from bone and abalone shell and how to make harpoons with detachable points that could be pulled in once a large fish or an otter or seal was hooked. No wonder the people here were often so tired of seafood. Sometimes, Child imagined how nice it would be if the village traded with their nearest inland neighbors, the Sa'aqtik'oyans, again. If only my father, she thought, were not so foolish and so stubborn.

She made the best of it. She had friends among the children, Squirrel and Otter, of course, and many of the others. She seldom had time to miss her friends from Sa'aqtik'oy, but she wondered at times what became of Sunflower. Crab was here. He seemed not to be interested in any of the Wene'mu maidens. It seemed so terrible for them to be kept apart.

How was Little Fish making out? Was his father pleased with him? In a way, Child was glad she did not have to try to satisfy him. As far as her mother was concerned, she was not even supposed to know that he was her father. He was a hard man. No wonder Pretty One seemed sad so much of the time.

Among the other things Child learned was how to make a fire and how to cook mussels and clams and oysters in a pit lined with seaweed right on the beach. She spent much time there, watching the sea and thinking. She even learned, after an inland expedition, how to make acorn gruel and how to make cakes of it by

33

frying the thick gruel on a flat piece of steatite close to the fire. The cake did not stick to the stone and it could easily be turned over and fried on the other side in melted rabbit or seal fat.

It did not require joining a guild to learn the art of storytelling. For once, she did not have to ask for an apprenticeship. It was in the storyteller's keesh that the children gathered on cold and rainy days. Child sat with her two younger cousins, Pearl and Butterfly, at her knees. They were toddlers when she first arrived at Wene'mu. Now, Pearl was six and Butterfly was five. They were the daughters of Seahawk's younger wife.

The boys liked stories too, the way Crow Eyes told them. Otter sat with his friends. He was ten now, two years older than Child. He was old enough to go out with the men to fish.

Even the adults came in at times to listen to the tales Crow Eyes told. Everyone sat around the fire listening to the old woman with her gray hair and long nails; she had a voice that was just right for stories of long ago.

Crow Eyes spun tales of the First People to inhabit the world, before the time of the Great Flood. Some of the First People ascended to the heavens to escape, like Eagle, the great bird of heaven, and like Sky Coyote, who knows everything and has great magic when he's not being too foolish to use it.

"Among them," Crow Eyes related, "lives Sun, who travels the sky in the daytime carrying a slow-burning firebrand in his hand. We need him, for light and warmth, but sometimes he can be very cruel. He catches people while he takes his rests during his journey. Then, when he goes home to his crystal house at night, he gives them to his two daughters to cook for supper. His daughters

34

are so very ugly, they wear rattlesnakes around their middles for aprons.

"In the Lower World are the Nunasis," she continued. "They are terrible monsters. Even though their homes are in the Lower World, they come up to our world when they become hungry for naughty boys and girls." She said this in a voice that sent shivers down the backs of children who were lazy or misbehaved in other ways. Pearl and Butterfly moved closer to Child. She found their hands and squeezed them reassuringly.

Otter grinned defiantly, but Child wanted to know more. "What do they do, these monsters?" She asked because she knew Crow Eyes was waiting for the question.

"I'll tell you so you'll watch out for them," she warned. "You may be walking along in the mountains one day, and see a pretty path that seems to beckon you into a grotto of trees beside a pond. There, you may find the Scorpion Woman. She will sing to attract you and you will want to hear her song, but I warn you. If you get too close, she'll sting you with her terrible tail and throw you into a basket to cook you." She made a motion with her hand like a scorpion's tail striking.

"Some of you have family in the villages on the islands where the Michumash live. If you go there, you may see the Haphap. He was once a wot of a village on the biggest of the first four islands. Its name is Limuw. He became a Nunasis in the underworld after he died. His mouth is like a canyon that opens in an earthquake. He inhales rocks and trees and even the trail you stand on. Watch out for him."

"What Nunasis live near Wene'mu?" Child asked. "I want to see one."

"Are you simple in your mind?" Otter interrupted. "Old Crow Eyes is telling us what to watch out for and you want to see a Nunasis up close."

Child shrugged. "I just want to see one. I'll hide so it won't see me."

Crow Eyes grinned, the missing places between her teeth giving her smile a menacing look. "So you want to challenge a Nunasis, do you, Child? Only half a day's journey from here, if you know where to look, in a secret valley lives Old Woman Momoy.

"She is a wild woman without a village and without laws to live by. She was once human like the Haphap, but she's a wild woman now. Her hair is like snakes. If she can catch you, she'll feed you magic flowers that will make you dream very strange dreams. Not only that, but she has magic eyes that can see right into your mind. She'll know what you're thinking, so you can't plan how to escape."

"She doesn't sound so bad to me, if all she does is feed you flowers that give you dreams," Otter said, dismissing at least one of the threats lurking somewhere out in the mountains. "At least she doesn't eat people."

"They say she eats nothing but tobacco." The children laughed. "But do you want to spend your whole life dreaming and doing nothing else? Do you want to waste away to a skeleton because you never eat?" she asked sweetly.

"No," he admitted. "I didn't think of that."

The storytelling went on longer, but before it was done, Child could tell the talk of Nunasis was frightening Pearl and Butterfly. She wrapped them up in their capes. It was cold outside away from the crackle and glow of Crow Eyes' fire, but it was a short walk to the large central keesh after their visit to the midden. They would soon be warm again.

"Don't worry about Nunasis," she told the girls. "I'm sure they never come into villages. I think that old Haphap is nothing but a real earthquake and Scorpion Woman is only make believe too. A woman can't have a scorpion's tail. Crow Eyes makes up stories to make children behave."

"Don't you believe Nunasis are real, Child?" Pearl asked. "I do. I'm going to be good and work hard."

"Well," Child admitted slowly, "maybe I believe just a little in Old Momoy. I don't like rules either, but I don't believe her hair is snakes or she just eats tobacco. Ugh."

The girls laughed. "Now hush. The grown-ups are probably sleeping." The three girls ducked into the entrance silently, unnoticed by its inhabitants.

Cloud Woman, Seahawk's first wife and Otter's mother, was pregnant again for the first time in ten years. She was talking to Full Basket, mother of Butterfly and Pearl.

"This keesh grows too small. Otter and my new baby, you and your two girls and our husband, that makes seven. Pretty One and her Child are nine. Why can't Seahawk's sister accept an offer of marriage. I know she's had several. If she moved out, there would be enough room. Isn't anyone in Wene'mu good enough for that woman?"

"Probably not," Full Basket replied. Animosity colored her voice, giving it an unpleasant, whining sound. Child stared at her and held her two cousins back. "I have not told you yet, but I think I'm going to have another and that will make ten of us in here. Something must be done. Seahawk must order her to accept a new

37

husband. She's his sister. He's wot of this village and she must obey him."

Pretty One stepped out from behind the mat that separated her tiny section of the keesh from that of the two wives and their families. Full Basket gasped. Cloud Woman glared at her. "How long have you been hiding there?"

"I have not been hiding," Pretty One answered coolly. "I live here. So do our children." She nodded toward the doorway. "Showing how selfish you are is not setting a good example for them. Come, Child."

Child left her cousins. She threw an angry look toward her two aunts and followed her mother into their section, closing the mat behind them. They had their own fire. Their home was actually a small keesh connected to the larger one by a tunnel. Despite its smallness, Pretty One kept it clean and pleasant. She swept her floor and scattered it with clean sand every few days. She not only cared for her own hearth, but she wove all the baskets and mats that the three families needed.

She made sleeping and carrying cradles for the new babies of the village, not to feel she was accepting charity when she dipped into the common cooking baskets, since she did not have a husband to put meat or fish there. Still, her brother's women made it clear that they resented her.

Child and Pretty One whispered long into the night. There were many things to talk about, things that both had been holding back. "I know you have not been happy here in Wene'mu, Mother," Child said after a while.

Pretty One sighed. She rubbed her weary eyes, which

often hurt her from the constant weaving and the wood smoke. "My brother has been good to us. I see that you're learning so much and the children here like you. I have enough if you are happy. All in all, Wene'mu has been good to us."

"But you were happier in Sa'aqtik'oy." It was not a question. "You had friends there. I remember." Pretty One did not speak, but she rubbed her eyes again. Child guessed that she was crying.

"You weave too much, Mother. I should help you. It hurts your eyes." She saw her mother's grateful smile and went to embrace her. "Oh, Mother," she said when they drew apart. "Maybe you should get married again. Maybe it would be good for you."

Pretty One was startled. It was a thing they had never discussed, nor had Child ever before mentioned her mother's marriage. Of course, she would know. People spoke about what did not concern them; but Pretty One hadn't wanted her daughter to be hurt.

"Do you know, Child, why we lived alone in Sa'aqtik'oy and why we live alone here, even though we are in the keesh of your uncle?"

Child nodded. "Yes, Mother, I know," she said. "My father divorced you and he wanted nothing to do with me because I am a girl." She had accepted it long ago. She no longer felt the sharp pain in her throat and eyes she used to feel when she thought about it. As an oyster develops a smooth pearl to protect itself from a grain of sand or irritation, she had put the rejection away and sealed it off.

She touched her cheek to her mother's. Pretty One still had the beauty that gave her her name. She was only in her twenties and was still a young woman, but there was something of age in her face, a look of resignation and disappointment. "You will be happy again, Mother. I will see to it."

Pretty One brushed her daughter's hair lightly with her fingers. "I'm happy with my daughter."

CHAPTER 6

Time went by slowly, but the seasons changed and Child grew.
Pretty One stayed in her section of
the keesh, unmarried. Perhaps Seahawk had spoken sharply to his
wives; they no longer complained
when Child or her mother were in
hearing. Even so, they were no
warmer than before, and Pretty
One often sat alone by her fire
while Child was working or playing.

One day, some of the children
were playing on the beach, engrossed in a game of shinny. It was
different than playing on grass, as
Child remembered from when she
watched the older children play at
Sa'aqtik'oy. Sometimes there, there
was an all-women match. Her
mother, Pretty One, had played

well, run fast, and laughed when she maneuvered the ball into her opponents' goalposts. There, the ball was made of skins sewn tightly together over a round stone. Here, it was an oval basket, lighter and easier to hit on the sand.

Child ran around two boys who were trying to block her and readied her shinny stick to slam the ball into her team's goal when a loud cry of gulls coming from high over their heads made her miss her swing.

"Stop," she said suddenly. "Look at the sky. It doesn't look right." Gulls and sandpipers wheeled and screamed as they made their way toward the mountains, away from the green-tinged and cloud-darkened sky. The foam on the crest of the waves looked unnaturally white against the water, and the wind rose.

The swells out where the precious boats and their crews lay were growing into house-size hills. Their nets kept them from drifting while they fished, but now they were trapped by them, unable to maneuver. Great waves crashed into the shore and grew larger even while the children watched. Lightning streaked from the sky farther out over the sea.

"My father is out there," screamed Pearl. "What will we do?" She began to run in circles, to the water and then back toward the group. "What can we do?" she repeated.

"Look," Child said, straining her eyes to see. "They're cutting loose the nets. Otter is in the boat with Seahawk and Crab is in the other one. They'll know what to do."

Several of the other children were terrified too, unable to do any more than watch. Already, their playing field was underwater and they had to back up to higher ground. Everyone had a brother or a cousin or a father out there.

"Quick, run to the village, Mudhen and Starfish!" Child had to shout to be heard. "Get everyone down here." Two of the biggest boys set off running hard.

"Now," she said to the rest of them, "we have to make long lines out of the broken nets that are waiting to be mended and then tie floaters to the ends. If we need to, we can throw them to the men and pull them in."

"But won't the men come in on the tomols?" a younger boy asked her.

"If they can," was her only answer. She looked out to the ocean, but it was hard to see. A driving rain began and the combination of the wind and the breakers was thunderous. Both the tomols were moving closer. "Keep working." At least she felt she was doing something, keeping the children busy at any rate. "Maybe these lines will help."

Every so often, another streak of lightning lit the sky to show them the boats and their crews struggling to keep afloat. The men tried to keep them heading toward where the children waited.

At last, the villagers came running, but they too could only stand and watch while the wind and the current tossed the two tomols up the crest of one swell and down into the valley of another while the foam washed over them. They were close enough now that men could be seen bailing water with their hands while the rowers paddled as hard as they could to get themselves out of the current, which pulled them strongly to where the beach curved out to a spit of land. There, the waves were already crashing over the rocks.

Some of the people tried shouting advice, although they could not be heard. "It's been years since a storm came in so quickly and so fiercely," one of the men said. In the sudden dark and rain, Child depended on her fingers to know the ropes by touch. She kept working to lengthen them and to attach the floaters. When she finished one, she laid it in a circled pile and began on another. The others followed her example.

An old woman came to watch. "Look what the children are doing," she called out.

Mudbird, a lanky man in his forties who no longer went out with the fishers, ambled over. His gray hair stood up like a kingfisher's crest at all times. Now, it was flying out in all directions, held up by the wind. His leg was once broken in a boating accident and it had healed crookedly. He functioned as Seahawk's spokesman and lieutenant in Wene'mu.

Unlike many of the others, he was not running up and down the beach straining for a glimpse of the men. He could not run anyway, but he, of all the men there, knew best the thoughts of the men in the boats.

"What are you doing?" he demanded of the group.

"It's to help," Child explained when no one else replied. "A strong thrower might be able to get the floaters on the lines over the waves so we can pull the men out of the water if they get washed overboard."

Mudbird understood her idea at once. "Good thinking, Child," he said, squeezing her shoulder. She beamed under the praise, but kept her fingers moving nimbly over the ropes.

The current was too strong and the waves too high. One of them lifted the farther of the tomols so high that it seemed to be suspended in air over the first. As one, the men in the lower boat jumped into the sea before the wave and its heavy burden could come crashing down on them.

Foam covered and concealed their immediate fate from the onlookers. When it cleared, both tomols were still floating, but hulls up, toward the shoals and the rocks. There were still heads to be seen above the water.

Mudbird went into action. He called with his loud voice to the hunters and the builders, the young men who had not gone out fishing that day. He called out over the sounds of the water and the wind and the laments of the women. "Take the ropes the children made. Throw them out over the waves. Pull the men in. We can still get our men to safety."

Child stood watching now among the others, hoping her plan would work. The strongest men stood as close as possible to the waves and threw in the weighted lines. There was no more she could do but pray.

Seahawk was the closest thing Child had to a father. Otter, her cousin, teased her sometimes, but she loved him too. Crab was like an older brother. She remembered all the times they laughed and gambled together. He never spoke to her of Sunflower since the last night she spent in Sa'aqtik'oy. He did not seem so very unhappy, but he had never taken a wife from among the maidens of Wene'mu. So many times, Child thought about Sunflower back in the other village and wondered whether she had married one of the young men there.

It must be that the wind and the rain are playing tricks on my eyes, Child thought. The woman standing alone with the baby on her back looks like Sunflower, only older. I don't remember seeing her here before. I thought I knew everyone.

It had been five years since Child saw her friend, but she carried a picture of her in her mind, of their last farewell. It *is* Sunflower!

She ran to the woman who stared out at the water to one man in particular, her hands twisting helplessly, but her eyes burning. She was mumbling prayers to Earth Mother as quickly as she could. By now, Sunflower must be about twenty, Child calculated. She must be an Antap priestess like her mother, Two Leaves, before her.

"Please bring him back to us," she said, not seeing Child standing near. "Make the wind stop," she implored. "Don't let the elye'wun pull him under the water." Those were the supernatural beings that lived under the sea who sometimes threw even whales onto the beach. She called on the sun to come out and on the earth by all of her names to make the sea behave.

One by one, men were pulled onto the beach to be received into the arms of their families.

"They'll get him out, Sunflower. They will. He'll come back to you." Sunflower turned and saw the girl at last. She looked at her as if she were seeing a ghost. But Sunflower herself must be a spirit, Child thought. She is at Sa'aqtik'oy even though she looks so real. She knew of the storm and she must have known Crab was out in it. She must have known because she loved him and she sent her spirit while she was in a holy trance to pray for Crab. But the baby cried. This could not be a spirit woman holding it.

"Child, is it really you?"

"Sunflower, is it really you?" The woman and the girl threw themselves into each other's arms.

"Let me hold your baby," Child said. "Crab is being brought in now. Run to him." Sunflower complied. Crab had just reached the beach, with the line looped under his arms. His mother and father had him in their tight embrace and were helping him to stand. He struggled to remain on his feet, breathing hard, sucking in great gasps of air. All around, mothers, fathers, children, and wives were holding on to their men.

Then Crab saw Sunflower. He gently disengaged his parents' arms and walked to her slowly, opening his arms.

"Crab. My love," Sunflower cried, and ran to him. "Thank you. Thank you for giving him back to me." She bowed her head to the earth.

They stood tightly together. When they looked up, Seahawk stood over them. Still holding hands, they looked back at him. Child, with the babe in her arms, was near. The truth told itself now. In spite of war, in spite of commands given, they were secretly wed.

"You have disobeyed me," Seahawk said harshly. "In the morning, you and this woman must leave Wene'mu." He turned away from the young couple.

Pretty One walked over to stand by them. Without saying a word, the two women embraced, then stood back to look at each other. After a while, Pretty One said, "Perhaps my brother will change his mind. If I have no influence with him, the priests might. We can appeal to them."

"Don't waste your breath, Pretty One," Crab said to her. He was breathing easily again, but his hair hung in wet clumps down his back. "I have been appealing to him for years. I *have* asked the priests to use their influence, but he's as stubborn as the wot of Sa'aqtik'oy. We must go."

"I'll go with you then. You'll need help with the baby."

"Into the wilderness with no village to protect you? I can't ask such a thing. Let me tell you what my life has been for years," Sunflower said. "My keesh is in a small valley not very far away, but hidden. Crab brings me meat and fish when he can. I gather alone for the rest of my food. Except for the baby, most of the time I am alone. I disobeyed Swordfish when I left my home. There is no village that will take us in. We are both outcasts now."

"I am alone, except for Child here. I would rather be with you."

"And Child. How does she feel?" Crab looked toward her. His parents had already told him who had thought of the weighted ropes. The girl would be highly honored here, made much over. She had friends in every home and every guild.

"I will plead with my uncle for you both," Child said. "It's not right for one man to have this much power. To exile a whole family because he is angry; it is wrong. The Antap should have a vote. If he insists that you go and they don't overrule his decision, I will go with you. I won't live in a home where there is no justice. We'll find a good place and start our own village."

"That's the Child I remember," Sunflower said. Before they left the shore, they looked again to the ocean. It was calm now. Gulls rode on the gentle swells, and the western sun warmed them with the last of its rays.

48

CHAPTER 7

Sunflower and Crab agreed to wait for them just outside the village. Child walked at her mother's side. On both sides of them, families stood and watched from before their houses as the two made for the central keesh. Mudbird and the children spread the word that it was Child who had thought to make the lifesaving ropes.

"Thank you, Child," were the words they heard most often as they passed. A few came up to them and handed them small baskets of acorn cakes. Crab's mother handed Pretty One half of a roasted rabbit. Pretty One thanked her in appreciation. What mixed-up feelings she must have now, Child thought to herself. She and Crab's father were thinking they had lost their son to the sea. Now that he was safe, they had lost him in another way. Exile.

They must have known about Crab and Sunflower all along. Did they know that Child and Pretty One intended to share their son's exile? They had other children here; otherwise, they would probably go as well. Child's mind was on her uncle. By her own decision, her fate was in the balance if they could not sway him.

They entered the main section of the keesh to see him reclining on his raised bed. He was covered with his furs. His wife, Full Basket, was kneeling beside him and handing him spoonfuls of the soup Cloud Woman had hastily warmed on the fire. Otter was sitting up, wrapped in furs by the fire and feeding himself. Both girls sat close to him.

Together, Pretty One and Child walked to within a stride of where Seahawk lay. Child waited respectfully for her mother to speak first, but before she could say a word, Seahawk interrupted the silence their entrance produced.

"I understand we have you to thank for many lives today, Child, my own included. Tomorrow, we will give a feast and dance before the gods who inspired you."

"Thank you," Child muttered. She looked to her mother.

"Brother," Pretty One said. She paused to swallow. "To thank the gods also, let us show forgiveness for all wrongdoers. Crab has always been devoted to you. Please, let him and his wife and baby stay with us. You won't be sorry. The Mother will smile on Wene'mu for your leniency."

"My sister," Seahawk responded, "our war with Sa'aqtik'oy is because Swordfish insulted our village, most notably you. Of all people, you must understand that the rules a wot gives to his people must be obeyed."

"But show leniency, Brother. They mean no harm."

Seahawk's eyes glittered like the sun upon water and a hard look came over his mouth. To Child he began to resemble her father. He was a man who held power over people and he relished it.

"A wot must have authority. Without it and the power to punish those who disobey rules, a village would be like a flock of sea gulls fighting over scraps on the beach. You have asked politely, with humility, as is your right. I'm sorry, but my answer is no."

"I am sorry then also, Seahawk," Pretty One returned just as formally, "but in that case, I'm going into exile with them." She backed away two steps, leaving Child standing before her uncle.

"Are you going with her, Child?" he asked her. "Because if you do, you will not be permitted to return."

"I am going, Uncle." She said it quietly, but the words sounded loud to her. There was no other sound in the keesh aside from the crackling of the fire.

Pearl and Butterfly jumped up and stood next to her. "Don't go, Child," they pleaded in unison.

"Sit down!" Seahawk glared at his two daughters. They meekly went back to their places. Child looked quickly over to Otter. He sat as a carved statue sits, his expression hidden from her. Did she imagine smiles behind the somber expressions of Seahawk's two wives? It was hard to tell.

"Think again, Child," Seahawk advised. "You no longer need to stay by your mother's side. You'll be grown in a few more years. You can make your own decision now. I would like you to remain. You belong in Wene'mu. Don't act foolishly."

When she hesitated, it was because she was thinking how to answer. He took the delay as indecision. "If it were anyone else, Child, I would not ask twice. I have loved you like my own."

His words gave Child what she needed. There were tears in her eyes. "If it were anyone else, I would have gone without explaining and without saying good-bye. It is my own choice to leave. Crab and Sunflower are not our enemies. Their only crime is that they love each other. I love you too Uncle, and I thank you for everything you've done for my mother and me. Good-bye."

She followed Pretty One through the entrance into their own section of the keesh. Child looked at the round walls of their small home. For five years, she had had her bed here. Her mother wrapped the rabbit and the cakes in skins and put them into the largest carrying basket. She rolled her bed furs and piled them in. Child took their bowls and cooking baskets, stacked by size, and packed them as well.

"Take our firestones, Child. We will have cold nights soon," Pretty One reminded her. "To start the fire and to cook."

Exiled. Child disliked the sound of the word. With all her brave talk, she had hoped it would not really happen, and that Seahawk would rescind his order. It is cruel and unjust, she thought to herself. It serves no purpose. She steeled herself not to cry again, and kept working, piling her bed furs on top of their other belongings. She and Pretty One put on their walking sandals.

"Take our digging sticks. We'll need them." Child

took a last look, then pushed open the skin that led to the outside.

Later, they all sat on mats around Sunflower's fire. She gave them each a shell bowl of acorn soup to have with their portion of rabbit. She already had packed all of her preserved fish and meat while they waited for the soup to warm. Several stitched skin bags of acorn meal stood ready for Crab in the largest carrying basket to carry along with his bow and quiver and his spear.

Sunflower gave them wooden mugs of mint and berry tea after their quiet meal. Then she smiled. The smile turned into a giggle and soon ripples of laughter washed away the gloomy thoughts from the small group in the pleasant little room. They all started to laugh. Even the baby laughed, his happy gurgling cheering them all.

"What's so funny?" Crab finally asked when he was able to stop laughing.

"My quiet, lonely little house." Sunflower gestured around them. "It's our last night here and it's filled with company." She laughed again, but Child guessed that there were tears inside that did not show.

They began early in the morning. Since Sunflower had a heavy burden basket between her shoulders, Child carried the baby, whom his mother called Cricket, on her hip. The others took turns carrying him while Crab went ahead with his bow and spear, watching for animal tracks.

Each woman carried a short skinning knife in her belt pocket. Even Child now wore the woman's skirt. Mother made one for her of pounded yucca fibers, and she had packed away another of tanned deerskin.

Crab guided them along the trail. The ground was hard to walk on after the previous day's downpour. Their feet sank in it. One of the times Crab waited for them, Child saw him standing thoughtfully, considering which of the meandering deer trails would be best for them to follow. Lower areas were hidden from their eyes because of the twists and turns of the mountains. There were narrow creeks and secret ponds, even tributaries of the well-known streams. They needed to make their camp within reach of water.

She reached him first. It was important to her that he know she intended to be a help, not a burden to him. He knew much more than she did. She was anxious to learn from him, to help him build the new home they all would share, and to learn how to hunt. None of the hunters ever allowed her to come along. She couldn't imagine Pretty One or even Sunflower drawing back the string of a bow, but perhaps she could get him to teach her.

"What are you looking for, Crab?" she asked.

"I'm studying the hoofprints of the deer who passed here. Their toes sunk into the mud. You can see." When she looked closely, he explained. "Her prints go deeper into the mud when she came away from her drinking place than when she went to it. If we follow these prints backward, we should find water.

"We must be grateful for the rain. Normally, this is fire season. The hot winds blow down from the desert in this month and the next. See how dry everything was before the rain?"

She saw yellow and brown all around them. Even the chaparral was dry and many pieces were broken from the rain. There were some dried raisins hanging from a wild grapevine they passed some time ago. She had picked what there was to throw into the acorn mush they would have for supper.

"You've never seen how fast a fire can spread when the chaparral is dry. A spark can set it off and fire can burn from the Big Valley down to the sea with nothing to stop it. It will go wherever the wind blows it. If not for the rain yesterday, I would forbid our making a fire until we had our shelter built." Child nodded, promising herself to remember what he told her. As far as she was concerned, Crab was their new wot and he was going to be a good one.

The others caught up to them. Pretty One put Cricket down. He walked a few steps, fell on his plump bottom, got up and walked a few more until he was off the path. He had his eye on a butterfly, but before he could chase it, he squatted and proceeded to expel the remains of his breakfast.

Sunflower laughed. "It's good to be young and not have a care in the world. I envy him."

Crab put an arm around his young wife. "So do I. I'm thinking about making a feathered banner to put here where we're going to turn off the trail, in case anyone wants to find us." He didn't say it, but Child thought she knew what he wasn't saying: *in case Seahawk changes his mind*.

"There's an oak a bit farther down the deer path. Let's rest there in the shade and eat."

Sunflower considered the food situation as they rested after their meal. "There are still acorns under this tree. We'll probably find half of the shells are empty or rotten, but if we work hard once we camp, we should have enough to keep us through the winter. We can also look for chia and of course there are bulbs to dig. We might even find some manzanita and gooseberries or some raspberries down near a creek when we find one."

"If I were to pick the month of my exile, I'd say this was a pretty good one," Pretty One said with a smile. It was important to keep up their spirits and to keep busy.

Before they stopped again, the sun was getting hot. Child felt the sweat dripping under her pack and Cricket was irritable. She heard the water before they saw it, a pleasant, whispering, rushing sound as the water from yesterday's unusual shower played over the rocks and pebbles of a stream bed that had been dry until yesterday. Then she saw the waterfall.

"I think we've found our camp," Crab said.

CHAPTER 8

The keesh was warm. Acorns, seeds, and roots were stored in raised baskets to keep them out of reach of mice or mildew.

Pretty One and Child were high in a meadow, looking for yucca. The versatile plant had numerous uses. The inside of its stalk was good to eat raw, boiled, or roasted. The roots were fine for food when they were cooked, but raw and pounded and rubbed with water, they became slippery and lathered into soap. The leaf points could be pulled out to make needles for sewing garments.

They sat in the meadow to rest after their climb on the warm day. Even in early winter, the rainy season, such days came often here. The ground grasses were long burned away and were slippery from an earlier rain. In a month or so, new growth would push up through the old, and the mountains would be full of new shoots and spring flowers.

"Child, I was wondering," Pretty One asked, "why you happened to pick the name Child for yourself. Was it only because of Seahawk's joke, that you were a dirty child that day?"

Child pursed her lips. One might almost see the thoughts and memories darting around in her head behind her intelligent eyes as she thought how to answer.

"To tell you the truth, Mother, it was a childish thought that made me choose my name." She smiled mischievously at the double meaning. "You see, I knew who my father was long before you thought I did."

"Even then?"

"I hoped just once, when he used my name, my father might call me Child."

"Oh. My poor girl," Pretty One whispered. She stood up and started toward Child, but a sudden rustling behind her made her flinch. She spun around. A cry escaped her lips and her hand went for the knife in her belt.

A wolf stood looking at her with slitted yellow eyes. The fur at his neck stood out straight; his tail was stiff, and he was growling softly.

"Mother!" Child shouted in distress. "Go away!" she said to the animal. "Don't you dare hurt my mother." The wolf took its attention from the woman and gazed curiously at the girl.

"Maybe if we just back up . . . ," Pretty One said uncertainly. "Maybe he's not hungry and he'll let us go." She stepped backward, one step and then another.

"No, Mother!" Child shouted too late. Pretty One stepped off the edge of a sharp incline and slid, then rolled over and over, down, until she came to rest against a clump of sage.

Child pushed past the wolf. "See what you did?" she asked it roughly, trying to figure the best way down. "Dear Chupu, don't let her be dead." She began to climb down the slope, holding on to vegetation and roots. She felt for footholds with her callused feet.

The wolf whined curiously, then scampered down also as if wanting to know what the strange pair was going to do next. At least Pretty One must have been right about one thing. The wolf could not have been hungry.

Before she could get to her mother, Child saw an old woman coming up the path.

"Dog? Where did you go now?" she said just within hearing. She looked behind her. Her white hair hung past her waist in long tangles, and she carried a digging stick.

"Dog! Dog!" she called. "Oh no. What is this?" The old woman saw Pretty One lying against the bush. She bent over her to feel her wrist. "Well, she's alive anyway."

Is she talking to the wolf or to herself? Child wondered as she made her way down. Some pebbles dislodged by her climbing made the white-haired woman look up. She saw Child.

"That's my mother," Child shouted. "What are you doing to her?" She could see now that the tangles of her hair clumped like white, coiled snakes from her head and that her basket was filled with entire plants ending in large white flowers. A fragment of a memory came back to her of sitting on a rainy evening around the fire in Crow Eyes's keesh.

"Who are you?" She reached the bottom and stood still, confronting the old woman.

"I'm trying to help your mother, foolish Tupnek," she answered. "That's my dog you have with you." The wolf ambled over to her and sat beneath her gnarled hand to be petted. "My name, Tupnek, is Momoy."

Child gasped. She had suspected it. A wild woman with white flowers and a wolf for a dog. The legend said she could see into a person's mind. Were all the legends of the Nunasis true then? One thing stopped her from running. Her mother was lying at the old woman's feet. "You keep calling me Tupnek. What does that mean?"

"I speak in the tongue of the North Country sometimes, the country of my youth. Tupnek means child. Now, let's see what we can do to help your poor mother."

Child held back her fear as she bent over her mother and put her ear to her chest. She heard a heartbeat. "She's alive," she said triumphantly.

"Yes. I know. I felt the beat in her wrist."

The girl looked at the old woman with incredulous eyes. "She has a heart in her wrist?"

"It echoes there, silly Tupnek. What we have to do is get two long branches to tie behind Dog here. He'll carry her back to my keesh so I can take care of her. Look, she's coming around now."

"Child?" Pretty One whispered hoarsely. "Oh, where am I?" With consciousness came the pain of her fall. She gasped as it shot through her leg. She was scraped and bleeding in several places.

With utmost gentleness, Momoy put her hands on Pretty One's twisted leg and felt it gingerly. "It's broken, daughter," she said. "Tupnek, hurry! Find those branches."

Child was back soon. She saw Momoy kneeling at her mother's side, the gray wolf waiting patiently only a few strides away. The branches she found dragged along the ground, making uneven ruts.

"There you are. Good," Momoy said brightly, standing up. She was stark naked now. Child noticed the muscles rippling on her spare frame. She would not have thought an old woman could be strong, although with no help but the wolf's, she must do everything for herself. She had no time for old age.

Child dropped the branches and ran to Pretty One. "Mother," she said, "are you going to be all right?"

Pretty One looked up at her daughter. Her limbs were straightened now. Her left leg was bound well in strips of Momoy's leather skirt, held straight with sticks. The old woman's waterskin lay close. With a rag from her ruined skirt, Momoy had wiped away much of the blood and the worst of the grit Pretty One collected during her fall.

"I'm much better already, Child." Even her voice was a little stronger. "Daughter, do everything Mother Momoy tells you to do. Help her bring me to her house. Then go and get Crab and Sunflower."

After all she had heard from old Crow Eyes, it was impossible for Child not to feel suspicious of the old woman, especially since she had seen the mysterious white flowers in her basket. But Momoy had destroyed her own skirt to help a stranger. Pretty One called her "Mother Momoy." What would Crab and Sunflower say? she wondered.

Under Momoy's direction, the branches were made into a serviceable travois, held together with leather thongs from a pouch within her basket.

"You come from the coast," Child observed, recognizing the knots that held the travois together as net makers' knots.

"Everyone knows how to make knots," Momoy hooted. Then, "But you're right. I lived with the Michumash for a while."

"Near the Haphap?"

"Of course, Tupnek. I played with his daughters and helped them catch children to cook for their father's supper."

"You're teasing me. Aren't you?" Child asked, looking to see if Momoy smiled at her joke.

"Of course," she replied, but she was not smiling. "Now, help me lift your mother. I'll get her back. You support her legs. Don't drop her left leg; you'll make the break worse. Very gently now."

"This will only take a moment, Daughter," she said softly to Pretty One. "Soon, you'll be still again. In my house, I'll give you some syrup I make from my flowers. It will help you sleep and relieve your pain so you can heal. Carry the baskets, Tupnek."

Child did as she was bid. They settled Pretty One on behind Dog and Momoy tied her fast to the travois. She led the wolf slowly, being careful to go around bumps. She and Child removed small branches that lay on the path. The girl heard what Momoy said about the flowers.

It was true then, but was it true the way Crow Eyes said or in another way?

Momoy's house was not far. It was made of tule reeds, much as all houses were, but it was not built well. A woman alone could only do so much. Maybe Crab and Sunflower could help her build a better one.

"Grandmother!" she exclaimed when she saw the straight rows of flowers and plants all around the keesh, with a path carefully laid out between them and going to the doorway. "How did you do it? How did you make them grow like this?"

For the first time, the old woman smiled to her. She still had her teeth. Even though her eyes crinkled up when she smiled, there was still the sparkle of youth in them.

"You called me Grandmother. That is right. You are one of the smartest tupneks I've met in a long time. Now, help me bring your mother inside. Then you can run and get your friends. I'll tell you about my garden later."

It was close to sundown by the time Child was back with Crab and Sunflower. Sunflower had Cricket on her back, his legs dangling from the woven support. Soon, he would be too old to allow himself to be carried.

Both Crab and Sunflower stared in amazement at Momoy's rows of plants. Sunflower set Cricket down, but she grabbed him again with a shriek as soon as she saw the wolf.

"He's Grandmother's dog," Child explained. She won't let him hurt anyone. I hope. Momoy is strange, but she's nice."

"I heard the legends too," Crab said. "She admitted she was going to give your mother flower syrup."

"She doesn't eat people. I just know she doesn't. She only teases. Grandmother?" she shouted.

Momoy came out. She was dressed again, and this time her hair was put up into a topknot arranged around a bone hairpin. A carved staff was in her hand.

"You are Antap," Sunflower said respectfully, walking closer. She stopped and inclined her head before she looked again at the old woman.

"I was," Momoy answered. "Like yourselves, I did as I wished and as in your case, it annoyed certain people. Like yourselves, I was invited to take my things and go."

"How could she know that?" Crab tried to whisper to Child.

Momoy turned to him. "I have very sharp hearing. I hear what you think before you speak."

"Ai!" Crab began to back away.

"Or else, I see a young couple with a baby and two friends without a village and I guess. Did I guess accurately, Crab?"

He jumped when she pronounced his name. "Mother told her your name before," Child said to calm him. "She's teasing you the way she teased me."

Momoy grinned. "My granddaughter sees through me. A smart tupnek, she is. Go see your mother, Tupnek."

To Crab and Sunflower she said, "You are welcome to spend the night in my keesh. I have food."

"Flowers?" Sunflower asked. She had heard the legends too.

"No. My datura flowers are only for those who are hurt or sick or those who need to speak to their dream helpers in visions. I have food you know and food that will be foreign to you. Sleep here tonight, you and your baby. My dog will hunt tonight so you have no need to fear.

"Tomorrow, if you wish, you may move to my valley to be near Tupnek and my daughter while she heals." She pointed a short distance away to a small pond they hadn't noticed before. "But not too close. Over there. I need my room."

CHAPTER 9

Momoy explained what she called
a garden while they had their evening meal. "I am very wealthy. I
have more strings of money than I
can spend. Now that I'm old, I don't
like to leave my valley, but people
come to me. Traders come through
from all over. Yes, they know how
to find me. They've been coming
here for a long time. They come
from the south and from the east,
from the cities. People live there in
ways we can hardly imagine here
in our mountains."

"What are cities?" Crab asked.
He handed Cricket a bowl of acorn
mush. The baby ate with two fingers now, like the rest.

"In the cities, there are many
people, far too many as far as I'm
concerned. They don't have

enough reeds to make themselves proper houses so they build houses out of stone. If the stone is too far away or too heavy, they make stones out of grass and mud." She made a rectangular shape in the air to indicate a brick. "Their houses are flat on top so the people can build houses on top of other houses; or so they tell me. Since there are so many of them, and they are always building, they're too busy to gather their food the way normal people do. So they make it grow right where _____ ___ ___ near their houses."

in't this anger the Mother?" Sunflower
ining in the Antap cult did not make men-
g the earth.
he peoples beyond the Mojave, live the
he Hohokam, and the Basket Makers. Their
me the Mother of All sent them a Corn
of her own daughters. This Corn Woman
lem all at different times. She showed them
t and use this." She pulled down a sack from
ened it, and poured a pile of corn into her

at is it?" Sunflower asked. Her eyes sparkled
ity. "May I?" She extended her hand for them.
want to see, Pretty One?"
)ne, who was sitting up on the bed Momoy
ed for her, with her leg out straight before
1. "I have seen. It's called corn."
rnels were hard and smooth in shades of yel-
e, red, and brown. A few were even bluish
eds, huge seeds is what they are. I've never
ı seeds. When we scatter chia to thank the
ır our many blessings, we know she will pro-
e for us."

67

"Yes," Momoy said. "You've learned what the Antap know, what all would know if they observed. Seeds make more plants. But these seeds are special, these and some others they gave to me. These are not for our people. The Chumash have no Corn Woman. They only have Old Momoy if they know where to look for her."

She paused to look around at all of them. Child felt as if a wind were blowing. Her hair felt tight against her scalp and little bumps stood out on her arms. It was warm, but Child shivered. In the small keesh, the fire did not waver.

"These seeds grow for me, where I bury them. The traders bring them to me for my flowers. But the seeds of these new plants in my garden here are for me and the people I give them to only. They must stay in my valley."

Crab and Sunflower bowed their heads to show Momoy that they accepted her injunction.

"Look!" Momoy threw the kernels in her hand onto the hot stones by the fire.

Why did she do that? Child wondered. Why is she burning the seeds? She looked to the strange old woman she had begun to call Grandmother without knowing why. It had seemed only natural. Momoy expected it.

"What are you doing? They're going to burn up," she said aloud.

Momoy only pointed one long finger. They all heard what sounded like green wood crackling on the fire and popping. The kernels jumped into the air and changed. Momoy caught them where they fell and handed some to each.

"Like flower buds," Child said. Cricket put his right into his mouth before Sunflower could stop him.

"Let him," Momoy said. "It's good to eat. That's what I made it for."

The next night, Momoy gave them soaked corn mixed with beans to eat with their roasted meat. Crab and Sunflower ate at Momoy's fire every night as the winter passed. No traders came that year, to Child's disappointment. She wanted to see how different people, people from cities, looked and sounded.

By spring, Sunflower was expecting a new baby. Child thought excitedly to when she would give birth. It was so long since she had seen anyone new.

Crab and Child were returning home late one afternoon after a successful hunt. The girl had grown taller. She was as tall as Sunflower now and nearly as tall as her mother. She had her hair tied up and back behind her so it wouldn't get in the way. The bow Momoy made for her was over one of her shoulders and her quiver with its five feathered arrows was on the belt at her hip. She had only needed one shot to bring down the yearling buck, and was proud of herself.

She brought in as much meat as Crab now. He never objected to teaching her how to hunt, and she was grateful. The two butchered the deer and piled the meat high in their burden basket to bring back. They were almost to the valley when a young man stepped out before them.

"Meat," he said happily. "All Momoy ever wants to give me to eat is acorn mush or that strange concoction she makes with her foreign foods. Meat is what I want. Nothing else fills me up. I'm so hungry. I'm always hungry. I'll help you carry that if you'll share it. Where are you going?"

He looked as if he hadn't eaten much for a long while.

He wore a sweatband around his long, unkempt hair. His eyes were big in his thin face and his arms were bony.

"Who are you?" Crab asked.

"Why, I'm Coyote. Everyone knows me." He looked carefully into their faces. "You don't know me?" He said it as if he couldn't believe it. "I guess you don't. I don't know you either. What are you doing here? Does Momoy know you're here?"

"I think," Crab said, "it would be a good idea for us to go to Momoy's house."

Before the sun went down, they were all sitting in front of Momoy's keesh, near the curing racks where Momoy's tobacco leaves were drying. It was another of the plants she cultivated. She chewed it sometimes, but today she had a tube of tule grass in her mouth stuffed with the chopped, dried leaves. She called it pespibata instead of tobacco. It was another of her North Country words. With a twig, she brought fire to the end of the tube and sucked on the other end greedily. She threw the twig into the fire and exhaled smoke from her mouth and nostrils.

"Coyote is my messenger," she said. "As long as Sa'aqtik'oy and Wene'mu call me Nunasis, I won't deal with them. If I did, you would know Coyote. He goes all over for me to bring my flowers to the villages to initiate the young people into adulthood."

"You can see what the result is," Coyote said between bites of deer liver that was baked on the hot stones before the fire. "Their wots are feuding. Even the Antap can't get them to make peace. It has something to do with a sister of one of them being divorced over a baby girl or some such nonsense. It's so stupid. A girl can be as good as a boy. Look at Child here. I heard she killed this delicious deer."

Child said nothing. Crab and Sunflower looked at each other strangely and Pretty One choked on the piece of meat she was chewing. Momoy went to pat her on the back.

"Are you sure you got that story right?" Momoy asked.

"Well, with gossip being the way it is, I can't really be sure, but I do know this: The children aren't being initiated into adulthood properly and they're very confused. Now, if they followed Momoy's teachings, everything would be better and I wouldn't have to travel so far for a decent meal. Is there any more?" he asked, holding out his bowl.

Momoy put more in his bowl. Child was fascinated by the way Coyote talked, but even more by the way he ate. She never saw anyone else eat so much at one sitting and still be so thin. She wanted to laugh at him; he was so funny. He saw her trying hard not to laugh and having a hard time at it. He winked to her.

She winked back. So, he wanted to play, did he? "That's my deer," she said. "You know I killed it. You can't have it all. Sunflower needs meat to help her new baby grow." She cut off a piece with the edge of her skinning knife and brought it to her friend.

"You're spoiling me, Child," Sunflower said. "I can still get up and get my own if I want more. You eat this. You work hard."

"He would have taken it all," Child answered, but she settled back on her mat and ate her extra portion.

Later, before she fell asleep, Child noticed the moon

shining through the smoke hole. She heard what sounded like the wind sighing in the trees, but there was no wind. She went out to explore. Not far away, she found Coyote sitting cross-legged on a rock in the moonlight, playing a song on a reed pipe. He saw her walking toward him, but he kept playing until the song was finished. Then he put down the flute.

"Well?" he said, letting the word float between them.

"Well, what?" Child answered after a while.

"Well, do you believe she's Nunasis or don't you?" Coyote asked her.

"She *is* different," the girl allowed.

Coyote let out a howl of laughter. "I like her anyway. I don't care what she is. What are you all doing here? She won't tell me. Did your village throw you out?"

"Hmm!" Child sniffed. "I don't have a village. I left by myself."

"How would you like to go exploring with me then?" Coyote asked in an offhand way. "You're pretty good with a bow and arrow. I won't have to go so long between meals and you can help with the carrying. You'll get to see new countries, have adventures."

Before Child could consider what he said, there was a hand on her shoulder. "She's too young to go anywhere with you, my lazy Coyote." It was Momoy, of course. Child wondered how she managed to walk up to them so silently that neither heard her come.

"You can do your own cooking and your own carrying. I never saw such a boy for being lazy."

Coyote smiled and raised his flute to his lips again. "She might, you know," he said before he blew into it again.

"Go to bed, Tupnek," the old woman said.

Only once more did Child have a chance to speak to Coyote alone before he had to go. "Did you really mean what you said about girls being just as good as boys?" she asked.

"Sure. Why not?"

"When I'm older, maybe I will make a trip with you," she said.

The idea of seeing faraway lands preyed on her mind. She tried to imagine many people living together in stone houses piled one on top of the other as she had heard in Momoy's stories. It would take a great deal of food to satisfy so many people. Did they have different words than Child knew? Momoy sometimes used words from where she called the North Country. If they all talked differently, then how could she talk to them when she got there? She began to believe she might go see them someday. Momoy didn't forbid her; she only said she wasn't old enough.

"When will I be old enough?" she asked Pretty One a few months later, "to go traveling and see the world?"

Her mother looked at her as if she was seeing her for the first time in a long time. She had grown again. She was taller than Pretty One now, like her uncle and like Swordfish, although she didn't like to think of that. It was eleven winters since her birth now, but she was still slender. She had none of the roundness of coming womanhood. Her body was strong for a girl, her arms and legs muscled and her step quick and graceful like a young mountain cat's.

"Why do you want to leave us, Child?" Pretty One asked somewhat sadly. "Aren't you happy here? Don't you like to be with Crab and Sunflower and Cricket? Don't you like to talk with me and with Momoy?"

"Yes," the girl admitted. "I do like all of you and I like to be with you. I'm glad Crab taught me how to hunt. I want to stay until after Sunflower has her new baby, but I want to see things. I'm not going to stay in this valley forever. I'm not one of Momoy's plants."

"She's right, you know," Momoy interjected. She had joined them. "Tupneks grow up and we have to let them. You know that, my daughter," she said to Pretty One. "Don't you?"

Pretty One bowed her head. She never argued with Momoy.

"Wait until your body starts to change. You'll need your mother then. After you have your first bleeding time, I will initiate you myself into adulthood. You'll see then where your future will be."

CHAPTER 10

Child had not eaten for two days. All she had had since then was water. The days were short. It was almost winter solstice, the anniversary of her birth. Sunflower's baby was born. Since then, Child's first bleeding time had come and gone. She was indeed glad that her mother was near to answer her questions and to teach her how to deal with the new changes in her body. One of the things she had learned while she lived in Wene'mu was that when a maiden had her moon flow, she must live in a special place, a keesh away from the main village.

"Aren't I supposed to go away and live in a women's house, or something, Grandmother Momoy?" she asked when she first discovered it.

Momoy was amused. "Where are you now?" she had asked.

"I'm here, in your house," Child answered, confused. She was trying to do what was right.

"I'm a woman. This must be a woman's house then." Child never thought about it that way, but it was a sensible way of looking at it. She wondered why the villagers she knew never thought of it that way. The time was finally here for her initiation into womanhood.

"Are you ready?" Momoy asked. Child sat on the floor of Momoy's house. Her mother sat watching on the platform bed nearby to be able to give Momoy and Child any help they might need. Pretty One was being trained by the old woman to take her place. Everyone was satisfied with this arrangement. Child's mother was where she belonged at last. She was loved and doing as her spirit called upon her to do. Momoy was happy. Now, it was Child's turn to find her own spirit guide.

"Yes," she answered. "I am ready." Momoy took her specially decorated wooden bowl and put it to the girl's lips. Without hesitation, Child swallowed the bitter contents. For a while nothing happened. While she waited, Child brought back into her memory the three years since she and her mother left Wene'mu. She remembered their first home in the meadow near the waterfall before they found Momoy's valley.

Crab and Sunflower and their boys lived there again. Momoy's "dog" did not enter into the nearby valley without his mistress. Sunflower's mother and father arrived shortly before the baby was to be born so Two Leaves could deliver her own grandchild. She said a young peddler came by with some soapstone carvings for the priestesses. As soon as he heard her name, he signaled to her that they must speak privately. He told her where she might find her daughter.

A few days later, Crab's mother and father turned up. Friends were trickling in ever since, those who were unhappy with the judgment of their leaders. The peddler, whose name the newcomers did not know, described a wonderful valley, deep in the mountains, and told them how to find it.

Coyote has been busy, Child thought happily. She began to feel a bit sleepy. The potion was starting to work. Mother was speaking softly to Momoy, but one word seemed to take forever to leave her mouth.

"What's wrong with both of you?" she asked, but neither seemed to hear her. She got up and walked out of Momoy's keesh. Above the valley, a condor floated on the wind. He was suspended, unmoving in the sky.

Child wanted to ask him why he didn't move. The next thing she knew, she was floating beside him. "What's the matter with you? Did you forget how to flap your wings?" she asked, barely pausing to wonder how she got up there.

The condor regarded her through unblinking eyes. "I am flapping my wings," she felt it say. "What are you doing in the sky?"

"I don't know." Child turned around. She could see all the way down to where Wene'mu rested by the sea. She looked out over the ocean. There were the tomols floating lazily on the gentle swells, with their nets spread out between them. The Brotherhood of the Tomol built new ones since the storm, she realized. Her friends were all older now also. She missed them.

After a while, she turned to look the other way. The morning sun was still in the east. "Fly toward it," the condor whispered in her ear. "I was once there. It's a long journey over the mountains and the desert, but when you get there, you'll see beautiful cities. Nice people live there. They sprinkle cornmeal in their high places for the birds. Go and see."

Child did not feel the wind flying past her face. She did not feel anything. She could not even see her own body. It was as if she floated and the earth flew beneath her. She saw mountains and green valleys rushing past, then a long green valley and higher mountains with snow on their peaks. She saw she was over the desert. Cacti such as she had never seen in her mountains grew here. They looked like tall men with their arms raised to the sky.

Strange stone formations sprung upward from the desert floor. She saw a wide river. The river cut into the earth and formed giant cliffs and gorges as it tore angrily onward. Away from the river, she saw mesas and valleys. Then, with wondering eyes, she beheld a city. Over a large area, square white houses stood side by side. From a nearby river, narrow streams carried water into fields of standing corn. She came closer to the fields. Plants grew there that she never saw even in Momoy's valley. Oddly shaped orange fruit grew on huge vines. She saw rows of bushes bearing small flowers that looked like cloud puffs. I wonder what they use that for, she thought.

She recognized tobacco leaves. That was one of Momoy's favorite plants. She used it even more than the white flowers people thought of when they thought of Momoy. Once, Momoy let Child inhale one of her tubes of the dried leaves. But she cringed at the memory of its taste, which she had found bitter.

Up and over more mountains, across another river

to the north she floated. More cities of different kinds appeared below her astonished eyes. She saw several with houses built on houses. They had cleared and smoothed enormous playing fields with earthen banked walls around them for spectators. How wonderful to be able to play shinny here, she thought. She saw people working, clearing the silt out of the ditches that brought water to their fields. Did they actually make these little tributaries themselves? What wonderful people they must be to think of such a thing! The condor must be right about them.

Once more, the ground flew past her eyes. Here was a half-circular city still being built. There were wide trails leading up to it across the desert land, perhaps from other cities. Men put in the wooden post supports and laid in the sand-colored bricks the women and the children were making. There were stacks of dried ones near the working place. People brought water to mix with the sand and straw in things that looked like baskets, but were not. What were they? More women smoothed mud plaster over the bricks. From four levels of houses at the outside edge, the flat roofs descended to three, then two, then one and a great level plaza.

From here in the sky, she saw what might be a thousand people, as many as the stars she could see on a clear night. She turned away from staring at the city. There was a reason she was here. It was more than curiosity.

A solitary building stood on a hill across from the unfinished city. The sun reflected from its white stucco surface. She felt herself being pulled toward it. Then, she was inside in a covered circular pit under the open walls. It was dark down here, but she felt a presence, not of a living being, but of a spirit.

"Who are you?" a gentle voice asked her. A sense of happiness came over her. The spirit filled an empty place within her she had not known there was.

"I'm Child."

"Do you know why you're here?" the voice asked her.

"I was seeking something," Child answered. "I think it was you. Are you my spirit guide?"

"I'm the spirit of an old man who sleeps. In his dream, he prays for help to come to him from his native mountains. Are you his spirit guide?"

Child did not know what to think or what to answer. There was some confusion, some mystery here.

"I don't know," she admitted. "I'm not really here, you know. I'm far away, way over there in a valley near the ocean where the sun ends his journey of the day. I've never been to this part of the world, but I'll come if you want me to. I'll find you. I'll try to help you."

The spirit radiated happiness. "That's all I can ask for. I'll wait for you then."

"It may take a long time," Child told him. "It's very far. Will you still be waiting by the time I can get here?"

"When you come to me, you will be a woman," the spirit said, "but I will be here. The Mother will let me live that long at least."

"I must go now," Child said. She was lifted up. The sun was behind her now. Pink and violet streaks painted the western sky over the desert. "Good-bye," she called.

A white thread of cloud made a path through the air. She could see it sparkling like a trail of stars back to the west as the sun went behind the horizon. "Take me home," she said.

A moment later, she was back in the keesh of Momoy.

"Mother, Grandmother," she said as Pretty One and Momoy rushed to her. "I'm home."

Her mother hugged her. "Child," she said. "The first stars are in the sky. You slept all day. I was worried."

Momoy handed her a wooden mug filled with water. "Drink this. You should eat now too. Later, you must tell us what happened in your vision."

Pretty One went to put food in a bowl for her daughter. It was only reheated acorn gruel, but it tasted wonderful to Child. It was the taste of home, of her own mountains.

"Are you sure you understood him right?" Momoy asked. "That's the strangest thing I ever heard and I've heard of strange things."

"Yes, Grandmother. My spirit guide thinks I'm *his* spirit guide. He wants me to come to him so I can help him. He's going to wait for me in a little house on a hill near the third city I saw."

Pretty One looked at Child sideways for a moment as she considered what the girl said. Child was a maiden of thirteen summers now. She was no longer a child in any way, but her experiences were different from those girls raised in the villages. The only man she knew well was Crab, Sunflower's husband. Coyote visited occasionally during the years. He was a strange young man, unsettled and happy in his wandering ways. It always seemed like a holiday whenever he turned up in Momoy's valley. He played his flute and told his funny stories. He ate until his stomach was distended, then he danced to amuse them. Sometimes Child danced with him. He promised Momoy he would come and be Child's protector if she made a journey. Was this the kind of influence she wanted her daughter to be under for the next few years? It was in the hands of the Mother now, if Child had to make this trip. Pretty One sighed.

"Did this spirit tell you his name?"

"No. He only told me he was the spirit of an old man who was sleeping. When I find him, I'll know it's him."

Pretty One barely concealed a smile at the confidence of youth. "Did he say you must take another name? You are no longer a child, you know."

Momoy smiled one of her rare smiles. Pretty One had grown herself in wisdom if she was ready to let go of her daughter's childhood. Even now, the people in the village that Crab had begun in the meadow by the waterfall thought of Pretty One by a new name. She was spoken of with reverence when she went to teach their priests how to initiate the children and a few had begun to speak of her as Young Momoy to each other.

"The spirit told me that when I find him, I will be a woman. When that time comes, my name will be Woman. Until then, I'm Child, except when I'm Tupnek, of course." Child's smile was almost as rare as Old Momoy's, except when Coyote was around, but she smiled now. Her even white teeth in her tanned, bronze-colored face seemed to bring sunshine into Momoy's dimly lit keesh.

"I suppose, then," Pretty One said, "we must begin to make you thick-soled sandals and boots, and stitch up warm clothes and capes for the winter. Mother Momoy said the traders tell her it gets cold in the east."

The preparations began.

82

CHAPTER 11

Child awoke one morning to hear strange voices outside. Men were talking to each other in a language she never heard.

"What is it?" Pretty One asked her from her bed.

"It must be the traders!" Child washed her face and put on her leather skirt.

"Don't put on your cape. You're not leaving yet," Pretty One called, but Child was already out the door.

She saw Momoy and the men making signs with their hands. This sign language was something Momoy had been teaching her from the time she knew Child would make the journey.

Child tried to interpret. Momoy signed, "You must wait two days for my son Coyote to come."

Her *son*, Child thought. Is he really her son or is he her son the way I'm her granddaughter?

"One day," the leader of the traders signed back. "We must get to the desert before the passes through the mountains are closed with snow." The sign for snow was the same as the one for rain, but he shivered first. Child knew of snow. It seldom snowed in her mountains, but once it did and the children had been delighted with it. Could it really get deep enough to close mountain passes?

"Two days," the old woman repeated. "I am Momoy." She made the sign of a flower opening and pointed to herself.

"Two days," the trader agreed.

"You take my granddaughter, Tupnek," she signed then. She saw Child waiting in the entrance to her keesh and motioned for her to come forward.

"We do not take a girl. A girl cannot keep up with us. We go fast."

Child walked to stand directly in front of him, her eyes flashing anger. "I walk fast like you," she signed, pointing to him. "I hunt. You take me." The leader moved back. She wondered if she had frightened him. His eyes became more humble than they had been.

"Your granddaughter?" he signaled to Momoy. It seemed less like a question than an exclamation.

Momoy rose and put an arm across Child's shoulders. "My granddaughter!"

"We take her," the man agreed.

Whether it was she who had convinced him or Momoy's saying that they were related, there was no more arguing. Momoy continued her trading. Child relaxed

84

and felt free to look over the men she was going to travel with.

Their leader, the one who spoke to Momoy, was a man who might be in his late thirties. He was dressed, as were the others, in a smooth fabric, the like of which she had never seen. He had a little beard flecked with gray. His hair was cut straight across his eyes. All the men wore their hair the same way.

The leader's name was Tonkawa. Several of his men were standing nearby watching Tonkawa talk with Momoy. She was almost as tall as their tallest men. The people of the cities must be smaller than her people, but the men were well muscled. They had no dogs to help them with their carrying and every one of them had heavy packs. Their legs must be strong as well. She hoped she was right in thinking that she could keep up.

Coyote arrived late the following day, surprising Child, but only a little. "How did you know the traders were here already?" Child asked him.

"Momoy told me to come," Coyote said. "I sometimes hear her in my head when she needs me. We're going to have so much fun. What is there to eat?"

Child laughed as she told him. There was always plenty to eat in Momoy's valley. She was thinking as they walked that he was right. An adventure would be fun if Coyote was along.

Momoy and Pretty One made clothes for Coyote too while they waited for the traders. They both put their leggings on as well as their tunics. They had fur capes to use for the cold weather as well as to use for their sleeping furs.

Child bathed the day before and washed her hair

with yucca root suds. She asked her mother to cut her hair above her eyebrows, straight across her forehead, the way the city men wore theirs.

She and Coyote tied quivers around their hips and filled them with the arrows Momoy made for them. Coyote brought oyster shells to trade in the cities. "There's nothing they like better," he explained as he showed Child the perfect shells, "except for Momoy's powders. They come here for that. Their priests love the stuff."

"I've got plenty of that in one of my pouches," Child said. "But more important than trading is my chance to find my spirit guide. He must be nice. I wonder what he wants me to do. Oh, Coyote, I'm so excited!"

The morning of their departure, Momoy gave Child and Coyote piñon nuts in two small leather bags stitched with thongs to close them tightly. "Don't eat these unless you have nothing else," she warned. "Eat meat if you can find it. I know you can rely on your ability, Tupnek, and the sharpness of your eyes and the arrows I made, but these nuts will keep you and give you energy if you need it."

"Find your spirit guide and come home," Pretty One said softly, giving Child a last hug. "We'll be waiting." Child lifted her pack to her back and joined the line of traders. Coyote walked behind her.

At the top of the ridge, Child turned around and looked back. She could see Momoy's keesh small against the hill with the garden around it. Grandmother Momoy and Pretty One were working there as usual, but they paused in their work and looked toward the ridge, their hands shading their eyes. She raised one arm in farewell and they waved back.

"When do you suppose we'll be back?" Child asked Coyote.

"Oh, in a couple of years, maybe three."

They walked hard all that morning. Tonkawa and the others walked at an even pace, not running, but far from slow. They stopped to rest and to eat when the sun was past the high point of its journey. They ate the meat of an antelope Child had killed a few days earlier. She wondered if the men knew that she provided their lunch. They had pemmican for the desert, where game was scarcer and more difficult to catch.

The day continued warm. That evening, they came to rest near a stream. One of the men began a small fire with his firestones to keep away the night animals. The men roasted what was left of the fresh meat and one brought some over to them.

As she ate, Child wondered what kind of man would become a trader. They all looked older than Coyote, although the youngest of them was not much older. Did they have wives and children waiting for them to come home? She would have enjoyed speaking to some of them if she had been able to sign more than simple phrases in the sign language Momoy had taught her.

Coyote, his appetite satisfied, gave a contented belch and patted his stomach. Then he pulled his flute out of his pack. A few of the men came closer to listen to him play. His music tonight sounded like the gently singing wind.

The youngest of the traders, the man she had noticed before, glanced toward her with an expression of puzzlement on his face, which was lit from below by the gentle glow of the fire. After a while, he went back to his mat.

"I wonder what his problem is," Child murmured to Coyote, who lay on his back, his mat close to hers.

"Who knows?" he answered. "He may wonder if you belong to anyone. You are the only woman on this journey."

"Woman?" Child repeated, her voice rising a bit. "I'll be a woman when I find my spirit guide, but in any case, I belong to myself."

"I know," Coyote said with a little sigh. "We're going to start at sunrise tomorrow. Get some sleep."

The traders were an amiable group. They resembled each other enough that Child wondered if they were all brothers or cousins and if Tonkawa was the father of some of them.

Much of her life had been spent climbing up and down mountain trails and carrying burdens. The extra walking and sleeping in the open hardened her muscles even more. Tonkawa did not show any surprise after the second day that she was able to keep up with them. Anything might be possible with a grandchild of Momoy. They must know of Momoy even in the cities, Child thought.

The young man, whose name was Okala, came up to them the third night. They had been given permission to spend the night at a Tongva village in the Big Valley to the east of where Child's people lived.

The nine of them were put up in the house of the head man of the village, the man the villagers called their chief. Okala had asked him to translate since he spoke both their languages, he explained as the two walked up to her mat.

"One of my daughters is married to a man of Talopop—" He named a Chumash village. "You know of it?"

"It's the one near the rock pool," Child said. "A pretty place. Coyote told me about it." Okala looked annoyed at the mention of Coyote's name.

"I think he likes you," Coyote observed under his breath.

"What does Okala wish to say to me?" Child asked the chief of the village. She motioned for him to make himself comfortable. It was his house, after all.

Okala spoke. The Tongva translated. " 'I think you are very pretty.' " In an aside, he said, "I'm telling you what he's saying, but I agree with him." Okala spoke again. "I have dealt with Mongollon traders before and I believe I understand all his words. He says if you have no man, he would like to share his sleeping mat with you. If you please each other, he will ask you to be his wife when you reach his city. He wants to know what *he* is to you." He gestured toward Coyote. "What shall I tell him?"

Child considered for a moment. She glanced toward Coyote. He shrugged as if to say, "Tell them whatever you want. I'll back you up."

It would be easy to say Coyote was her husband. Young women, even ones as young as Child, often had husbands. If she said it, Okala would have to leave her alone. She expected to spend many more months in his company and it certainly would make things easier.

At last, she said to the chief, "Please, tell Okala that I am on a quest to find my spirit guide. I have no time for a man until it is done. As for Coyote, he is my kinsman."

The chief translated. Okala lowered his eyes. "Tell him also," Child continued, "that if I decide to take a man, it will be a man from my own people."

Okala spoke again.

" 'Since when does a young woman go searching for a spirit guide?' Okala is asking, but I want to know also," the chief added. "I never met a woman on such a quest."

"That is between my spirit guide and myself," Child answered. "Please be good enough to thank Okala for his offer. I will be happy to be his friend though, if he will teach me his language." She smiled sweetly to the headman. "Was it very hard to learn?"

The chief beamed at her flattery. "It is difficult, but you'll have time to work at it. I'll tell him what you said."

Okala listened, a growing look of sorrow on his face. He made ready to depart for his own mat, when Child put a hand on his arm.

"Ask him if he would like to play dice with me. I have these bone ones and I see you have a gambling tray. Would you play too? I have too many strings of money. They're weighing down my backpack."

Okala's mouth began to turn up in the corners and his eyes began to lose their sorrowful look. "He says he would be happy to. So would I," the chief said.

The four of them sat around his mat and threw the carved bones. Part of the game depended on where the dice fell on the tray, the other part on the number combinations. A certain amount of skill in gambling added to the player's chances of winning.

Before they were ready for sleep, Child had enough strings of money to cover her quarter of the chief's mat.

"I'm wiped out," Coyote complained. "Remind me never to play with you again." He winked as he said it.

"Thank you for the game," she said to the chief. "Now, do you think five strings of money should cover our debt to you for our food and for our sleeping here?" She handed him back five of the strings she had won.

He slipped them off her hand, smiling. "I wasn't going to charge you. It was my pleasure, but as you said, you wanted to lighten your load, not make it heavier."

"Perhaps you will let us stay with you again, when Coyote and I return, so I can win them again?"

"You can stay with me anytime, Tupnek." Child was glad she had decided to use the northern name. The Tongva chief did not know Momoy's dialect of Hokan and he did not know the name meant Child.

"Thank you," she said to Okala in careful tones in his own language. This much of it she had already learned during the few days she spent with the Mongollons. "Good night."

"Good night," he said to her, no longer unhappy. He went off to his own mat.

"The houses are very much like the ones at home," she whispered to Coyote. Their mats lay side by side and each was wrapped warmly in furs against the chill of the night.

"You were very clever," he whispered back. "I have to compliment you. You have the chief and Okala eating out of your hand, even though you won the chief's money and you turned Okala down."

Child smiled. She stretched against her sleeping furs and flexed her toes. It had been a good day. Then something occurred to her.

"Coyote, are you really Momoy's son?"

He scratched his head and turned to look at her. At last he answered. "I don't know. She brought me up, so she might be my mother, but she might have found me. Why does it matter?"

"Well, I was wondering. If you're really her son, then we really are kinsmen, aren't we? You're my uncle."

"Except for one thing. I'd be happy to be your uncle, but I can't because you're not really her granddaughter. Did you forget?"

Child giggled softly. "I guess I did."

CHAPTER 12

The next morning, they ate breakfast with their hosts. The wife and
daughters of the Tongva chief
poured water and acorn meal into
several cooking baskets. As at
home, it was the obligation of the
wot and his family to see to the
village's guests. They built up the
cooking fire. Firestones, a necessary ingredient to cooking, were
taken from the fire with sticks and
dropped into the cooking baskets.
As soon as the acorn mixture
stopped boiling, another stone was
added. The mixture was stirred and
kept boiling until it thickened.
Then, the gruel was ladled out into
serving bowls.

"Wonderful. Just like at home,"
Child commented to Coyote. She
thanked the Tongva women. As

soon as it was cool enough, she dipped two fingers politely into the bowl and ate. The Mongollons did not seem to be enjoying the food as much as she did. It must be that what you are used to tastes best, she thought. The only place they could get familiar food was in Momoy's valley. No wonder they liked her. These people are very much like the Chumash, except that they use other words and they live down here in the valley, where the air is so unhealthy. She watched the smoke from the cooking fires rise into the air and spread out.

"There are mountains on all sides of us here," Coyote commented when he noticed her looking up at the smoke. It's like a big basket. There's nowhere for the smoke to go."

"Doesn't it ever go away?" Child asked.

"When the desert winds come over the northern mountains, the smoke gets blown away, but those winds are strong. Also, rain can wash the sky clean."

"You've been in this valley before, haven't you?"

He nodded. "Momoy sends me many places. They honor her here also."

"They will in Wene'mu and Sa'aqtik'oy also some day, if I have anything to say about it," Child said emphatically.

After breakfast, they made their farewells and headed south. They walked for a long while before they stopped to rest. The trail brought them up into the green hills that separated the long valley from the ocean plains.

Halfway up the first hill, Child turned and looked back. A haze of smoke hung over the place. "You know, Coyote," Child said as she detached her basket water bottle from her belt to take a drink, "the valley is pretty and it is a nice place to visit, but . . ."

"Yes, he answered, looking back also. "I wouldn't want to live there either."

They slept in the mountains that night. Child felt more at home here than she had in the last four days. These mountains were part of her own. They sounded the same, the same plants grew here, and the stars were just as bright.

They woke, ate some meat, and set out again just after sunrise. This crossing took only a day. Once, Child did not hear Coyote's footsteps behind her. She turned in time to see him disappear behind some of the scrub brush. There was no midden between villages and people had to do what was necessary wherever they happened to be.

A short while later, he was back on line. Two rabbits were slung over his shoulder and he was cleaning off the two arrows to use again. He gave her his special Coyote smile. "I like fresh meat, remember?"

The view as they began the descent on the other side was spectacular. There was more flat land in one place than Child had ever seen before. How many days would it take to cross from the ocean to the eastern mountains? Child wondered. Even the traders seemed to be measuring the distances with their eyes.

The sea was far to their right. The mountains to their left were at least three days walking from here. Tonkawa spoke to one of his lieutenants. From what she understood of the conversation, they were trying to decide whether to go farther south before they turned east or to cross the mountains.

Okala came over to them to try to explain using signs, some of his language, and some of theirs.

"It is more days walking to go south." He pointed to

make sure they understood. "Maybe the mountain way will be faster, but there may be snow." They followed the gist of what he said to them, if not all the words.

"Tonkawa wants to think more. He say tomorrow."

"Thank you," Child said in Mongollon. They shared the rabbits with him that night while they continued their lessons.

Later, Coyote asked Child, "Why do we struggle to learn his language? Your spirit guide spoke words you could understand. He must be one of us."

"Is it possible?" Child asked. "I never thought of that. But maybe all spirits can understand each other."

"Maybe your spirit guide isn't in a Mongollon city anyway. You said you saw three kinds of cities."

"I'll find out which one it is by describing it to Okala later, when I can speak better."

It was getting toward evening again. Tonkawa was looking for a good place to camp. They had passed a river earlier and drunk their fill and topped their water bottles, but he did not want to stop while there was still light to walk.

Now, it was getting dark rapidly. He halted the group and sent four of his men to scout for a good place to make their evening camp. Child removed her pack and sat down wearily, resting her back against it. She wiped the sweat from her forehead and felt it trickle down her back, making her feel the cold of the early evening chill. She threw her cape over her shoulders.

She refused to complain about being exhausted. Tonkawa would say he was right not to want to bring a girl. She could see for herself that the men were tired too. He was pushing them too hard and too fast. If she were wot of these traders, she would give them all a day to rest. As it was, fatigue could cause a serious mistake, even before they reached the mountains. Of course, Tonkawa wanted to get through the mountains before there was snow. If it could get that bad, there was good reason to worry.

A yelp and then a cry for help startled her out of her reverie. She did not know the word he used, but anger and fear and soon terror were in his screams.

"Get me out!" she heard distinctly as she ran toward the voice. The others ran too. They got to a clearing around a pond. Near the pond's edge, they saw Sando, funny Sando who amused the others around their campfire, up to his knees and sinking. His struggles made him sink faster. He was getting deeper into it. "Find something to pull him out with," Tonkawa screamed. None of them had their packs. He looked for a branch or anything with which to help the struggling man.

Child pulled off her cape. She got as close as she could and threw one end of it toward Sando.

"Pull!" she screamed. He must understand. He reached for it. She tried to hold tight as he pulled, but she began to slip toward the bubbling water herself. The whole pond smelled from asphaltum. She could even see some of it black and shining at the edges of the pond. It was tar!

She saw Coyote running toward them from the corner of her eye. "Coyote," she yelled. "Help me!" He was behind her at once. By now, she was lying half over the false pond. He took her feet and tried to pull her back. It was not enough. The tar was winning.

"Everybody!" he bellowed in Mongollon. "Hold on! Pull us out of here!" All of the men were on the chain now, each grasping the waist of the man before him.

"Momoy, you've *got* to help us now," he muttered in Hokan. Only Child heard him. Little by little, they moved back until they were completely out of the treacherous tar pit.

Tonkawa rushed to Sando. "My son!" he cried, enfolding him in his arms. "My son." Then he turned to Child. "You saved him."

"We all did," she said.

"What do you want for it?" That was one of the phrases Okala taught her. She felt black mud oozing from her clothes and her skin.

She did not know the word for it in sign or Mongollon, so she said it in Hokan: "A bath."

Tonkawa shook his head and smiled. Her request was so obvious, he could not fail to understand, but there was nowhere to take one. In the dark, it might be fatal to move. They backed up and lay down where they were.

They had no packs and no food, but the last thing they wanted to do was fall into the tar pits. They could always retrieve their packs in the morning.

Child lay next to Coyote, as usual. She felt miserable and sticky, but she pulled her filthy cape over both of them to try to keep warm.

"Thank you," she said, "for your help."

"You're welcome."

"Momoy helped us too, didn't she?"

"Of course," Coyote answered as if it were no big thing.

As soon as it was light, all of them made their way carefully away from the pits and toward the trail. Child and Coyote heard the wailing and commotion before they saw.

"Our packs are gone," Okala called back to them. The traders were on the ground, feeling the impressions in the grass left by their heavy packs. They tried to find any sign to show what might have happened to their belongings. The result of more than two years of walking and trading was taken from them. Tonkawa looked about to cry. Suddenly, behind them was movement. They turned around.

About thirty men stood there. The traders gathered together into a tight group. They had no weapons and they were hopelessly outnumbered. All Child could think was that she would never see the cities, never be able to meet her spirit guide and find out what he wanted of her. What did these people do with their prisoners?

The man who must have been their wot stepped forward and spoke. Coyote answered him. He understood the wot's language. After a few moments, he returned to the group and explained in sign. They were in the country of the Topikars.

"Their wot says he's very sorry we didn't see their warning signs in the dark. They took our packs to their village for safekeeping. He invites us to go to their village for food and a bath." He spoke in Hokan as he signed to make sure Child understood all of it.

"A bath!" She began to laugh. "A bath!"

With Coyote's help, Tonkawa was able to speak to the wot of the village. It was against custom for women to sit in the temescal, the sweathouse where men bathed, but occasionally, when one was sick or in other special circumstances, exceptions were made. Tonkawa made a trade for the village's hospitality and for Child to sit in the sweathouse with one of the female healers, who would help her scrape off the tar.

With the woman's help, Child was able to get relatively clean. Spicy sage leaves imported from the mountains were provided by Tonkawa. Mountain sage, laurel, and thyme were highly prized by the lowlanders, so the Mongollons made sure to have plenty of it for trading along the way and for the citizens of their cities.

The healer sprinkled sage over the hot stones of the fire. First, the hot, scented air opened Child's pores. Sweat loosened some of the tar so the healer could scrub it from her skin. Then, the woman poured water over the fire. The small, earth-walled room, partially built into a hill and roofed with reeds, filled with steam.

Finally, the heat became too intense. Child and the healer exited the temescal. From a water basket, the woman poured cold water over Child, then dried her briskly with a towel made of woven grass.

The wot's wife wrapped a robe around Child and took her to her own bed to close her eyes and have a bit of a rest.

"The priests will purify the temescal so the men can use it now," she signed to Child. As grateful as Child was for the care these people gave her, she did not care to hear this.

"Have your people build another one for the women," she signed. The older woman looked surprised and puzzled, but she smiled politely before she left the house so Child could sleep. Child continued on her thought after the woman was gone. "Then, neither temescal would have to be purified."

When she awoke, the wot's wife was there waiting. She gave Child a new garment to put on over her head in place of the one that was ruined. The material it was made of was something new to the girl. She felt it. It was not as light as the trader's clothes. They wore several layers of shirts made from cotton. Okala told her the word for it and that he would show her the plant it grew from when they reached his home. This material was so thick and warm-feeling to her fingers, it might keep a person warm by itself except on the coldest of winter days.

"What is this made from?" she signed.

The woman shrugged and threw her hands up. Even if Child knew none of the complicated language of signs, she would have known that gesture.

"Your men gave it to us. We sewed it for you while you rested," she explained. Child thanked her. The woman left again while she dressed. Her original leggings were still usable. She folded the others and put them in her pack, which was left for her by the doorway.

She decided to walk out and try to find her companions. She had certainly held them up enough by falling asleep when she only intended to rest for a little while. After all, Sando was the one who had the real fright; he had almost been killed.

The houses looked very much like the keeshes of the Chumash, except that they were somewhat smaller and the weave of the tule reeds within their framework was slightly different, but not by much.

"There you are," a familiar voice said. It was Coyote, of course. He also wore a shirt of the warm, thick fabric.

"I'm sorry I slept so long. Tonkawa must be angry. I guess I'm not used to walking this much, but I didn't want to admit it because I told him I could keep up."

"I'll tell you a secret," Coyote said. "We all needed a rest, but the men wouldn't admit they were exhausted if a girl could keep up without complaining. If Sando weren't so tired and half falling asleep, he would have smelled the tar before he stepped into it. If we all weren't so tired, we would have seen the warning rocks these people put alongside the trail. When rocks are arranged in a triangle like that, it means danger. I didn't even see them myself. Now that we were all forced to rest, the men are grateful."

Child could hardly believe it. The foolishness of men sometimes amused her. She hoped Sando was all right now and that he was able to get the tar off. He had been in it a lot deeper than she had. That made her think of the new fabric.

"What is this made out of?" she asked as they walked. Coyote seemed to know where they were going and she allowed him to guide her.

"They call it wool," he explained. "It's very precious. Our Mongollon friends have been to Olmec territory far to the south. The Olmecs trade with people many months farther south of them. The people there take the fur from animals called llamas and weave it. Sando told me about it while you were sleeping."

"It's so tightly woven and so smooth and warm," she commented. "Do you know where everyone is?"

They reached the dancing and feasting place. It was very crowded. All the people inside were looking down the path as if they were waiting for someone to come. Food was laid out on mats. The day ended early this time of the year and it was beginning to get dark. Torches were already lit.

"I forgot to tell you," Coyote said. "This party is in your honor."

"Coyote!" She felt the blood rushing to her face and

her ears burning. She tried to step back, but Coyote pushed her in front of him.

Tonkawa and the wot of the village came to escort her to a mat in the center of the floor. Sando was there also, in new clothes. The highest priest held a twig to the fire. With the burning brand, he lit some dried white sage leaves in a large abalone shell. He offered the pungent smoke in the four holy directions. "We do it just the same way," she called to Coyote, but he put one finger over his mouth to remind her not to speak during a ceremony.

The priest placed the shell down. Then he directed Tonkawa to stand in front of him, facing the people. Tonkawa was holding a beautifully decorated basket, not much bigger than an eating bowl.

"Tonkawa thanks you for saving Sando," he said in his own language and in sign for the visitors.

"I wasn't the only one." She could not help herself from speaking. It was not right to take all the credit. She hoped she said it right.

Tonkawa spoke. "You ran fastest, you thought what to do. You risked your life." He reached into the basket and withdrew a necklace. It was the most beautiful thing Child had ever seen. By the torchlight, she examined it. There were shiny, yellow birds, as yellow as the sun, and green figures that looked like men, but their arms were much longer. All the figures hung from a thick chain. She expected a chain to be made of woven grass, but this one was made of the cold, hard stone that made the yellow birds.

"What is it?" She could hardly breathe. It was so beautiful. Could he really be giving it to her?

"Gold and jade from the south," he said. He put the necklace over her head. It hung halfway down her chest and sparkled in the torchlight. She murmured a polite thank-you.

Tonkawa motioned again. "I would like you to think of me as your father for as long as you remain with us."

This, Child understood. She covered her eyes to hide her emotion. She did not wish for the men to see her cry. "I have no one else I can call father," she said at last. She took his hands and put them to her cheeks so he could feel that she had been crying.

"I will call you by your name, but I will try to think of you as if you were my father. Thank you."

"And for the Mother's sake, tell me if you're tired," he said. He put one hand under her chin and smiled. "If you won't admit when you're exhausted none of us will get any rest. Now, it's time for eating and dancing."

Coyote played a lively tune on his flute. A drummer drummed a beat on a plank of wood laid between two rocks. The high priest said to Child, "We dance not only for you. We dance to honor Mother Earth. She is called Chupu in some places and Hutash in others. Here, we call upon her and upon Tugupan, the sky." He pointed upward to the stars. "As Hutash is the Mother, Tugupan is the Father. You must also eat and dance."

It was all the encouragement Child needed. She ate. Then she turned and leaped and moved to the music. Someone else began to play the flute, so Coyote could eat. Then he danced also. Only Coyote could leap higher to the music than Child. She slept well that night.

CHAPTER 13

As the time passed during their journey, Child felt more and more as though she were part of a big family with a father and many brothers. Part of the reason was that she was learning the language of her companions, but the biggest difference was how they all treated her after the incident at the tar pit. Tonkawa actually asked *her* if he was pushing the men too hard while they were sitting around their evening campfire. Child became used to rising before dawn. Now, she was getting used to walking until sundown. She watched the others. If any of them were dragging their feet or starting to doze while they walked, she suggested a break.

Child and Coyote were both

better hunters than the traders were, so during the mornings when they were allowed by Tonkawa to rest late, or during the afternoons they camped early, the pair went off to replenish the food stores. What was not needed was smoked for the mountain and the desert crossing.

The two were invited to sit with the rest around the main campfire. If Tonkawa became like a father to Child, the others became like brothers. Okala never looked at her as a potential wife after the ceremony when Tonkawa gave her the necklace. Of course, Coyote always retained his place as her special friend, the only one who spoke the same language. Tonkawa led them close to the eastern mountains, but they continued to walk south. They stayed several nights in the villages of the Cahuilla. To the traders' delight, the villagers gave them hominy made from corn.

"How can they have corn, Tonkawa? I thought corn only grows near the cities or in Momoy's valley." Child was able to use many Mongollon words by now and the Mongollon had learned some words of hers. They were able to communicate well enough.

"We taught them about Corn Woman here. They thank us by feeding our trading caravans. Tupnek, we are more than Mongollons. We belong to the pochetas, the Brotherhood of Long-Distance Traders. The pochetas have special rules. Our brotherhood gave Momoy corn in exchange for the powders she makes, which are valuable to our priests. Both the pochetas and Momoy had to agree to certain conditions before they could reach an agreement. The result was that no pocheta will ever teach anyone in your mountains about Corn

106

Woman. Only Momoy may use her teachings, since they are, in a way, sisters.

"You will not stay with us, but during the time you remain in my care, it is as if you were my apprentice into the brotherhood. I expect you to keep our rules now and forever. I mean this for you also, Coyote." The young man was listening intently to his words and watching his hands to make sure he understood in case Child needed explanations.

Coyote looked at Tonkawa with his big, dark eyes. "That goes without saying. You are master of traders as Momoy is mistress of her flowers. Your word is our law."

"Of course I agree," Child promised solemnly. "I never want to make you sorry you let us make this journey with you."

Before they went to lay their sleeping furs in their hosts' houses, Tonkawa motioned with the sign language that he wished to speak to the shaman of the village. He returned to his traders while they were still talking around the fire.

"Sleep late, my children," he said. "It's going to snow tonight."

Child slept with one of the families that night. A little girl of the family crept into her furs to join Child and to keep warm. The Cahuilla huts were small. They had few reeds to weave for walls and few willow or birch trees to use for framework. The thatch huts contained only sleeping places enough for each family, but the Cahuillas, like every other nation they had passed so far, gave hospitality to traders.

It snowed that night and all the next day. Child stood just outside the opening to the small hut. The little girl from the night before came up to her shyly and stepped under her arm.

Child held her hand out to catch some of the large snowflakes. "Pretty," she said. The word reminded her of her mother.

The girl watched the snowflakes melt on Child's warm hand. She giggled, then shrugged, not understanding Child's language. She pointed out at the white village. The houses looked like hills of snow, however much of them could be seen at all through the swiftly falling flakes. The girl shivered and giggled again.

"Yes, it's cold," Child agreed.

The Cahuilla girl took her to the village midden. Child was now grateful that she had two pairs of warm leggings to wear under her skirt. It must be colder still where they were going.

The heavy, gray clouds covered the sky all that day. Around the family fire, children came in to see the foreign trader woman with her hair cut like a man's.

Later, Child found Sando and Okala discussing the weather.

"Hello there, Brave One." It was Sando's new name for her. He spoke in Mongollon, but he'd told her earlier in sign what the name meant. "How fares our little sister?" Okala moved over to make room for her so she could warm herself by their fire.

"Is it so bad that I cut my hair like this?" she wanted to know. She ran her hand across her forehead where her hair hung over her eyes. The rest of her hair was tied back in one long braid. Most of the traders wore it the same way. It seemed quite sensible.

"It looks fine to me," Sando said, grinning.

"I wonder, though," Okala added, "what our mother

will think of you. You wear your hair like a man and you can bring down a deer with that big bow of yours faster than any of our hunters can. She'll think you're a very strange maiden, Little Sister Tupnek."

The next day, when the snow stopped, Tonkawa walked a short way from the village. Child watched him go. The sky was blue now, a sharp, bright blue. The snow on the earth and reflecting from the mountains dazzled her eyes. Where the sun shone on it, it sparkled as she walked.

When Tonkawa returned, he brushed the snow from a good-size rock and sat on it, facing west, with the sun at his back. His men gathered around him. From a pocket sewed on the inside of his cape, he pulled a folded piece of leather. Child watched curiously. The inside of the cured leather was light and had black lines marked on it. Tonkawa inspected it well. Then he held it up for the others to look at, tracing one of the marks with his finger.

"What is that?" Child whispered to one of the traders.

"It's a map. It shows where we will travel with some of the routes marked out, in a small copy as if from here to our home was this big." He measured in the air the rectangle of the map. "It is as if a high-flying bird were looking down and could tell us what he saw."

"Like the condor in my vision!" Child said. The trader looked at her in puzzlement. She only shook her head. She did not feel like explaining it. What a thought, though. Not to have to trust to memory!

"It must be very valuable," she said.

"It is to us." Mika, one of the traders, agreed.

"As valuable as this necklace?" She touched the lovely jade-and-gold circle she wore around her neck. People had been looking at it, even staring at it when the travel-

109

ers stayed overnight in villages along their route. She had taken to wearing it under her shirt, close to her skin, so as not to attract attention. Some of the looks she received were more than just innocent admiration.

"A thing is of value if it's useful. This map is useful. Without it, we might not get home," Okala said.

"But," Sando added, "to someone who never left home, it would have no use at all. Your necklace is pretty. To me, it's only pretty stones, although it took skill to pull the yellow rock away from the rock it grows in and to melt and shape it. The jade is also pretty and well worked, but I prefer our own turquoise. At home, a perfect shell may be worth just as much. They are given as prizes in our games."

"But I can pick up shells on the beach."

"Yes," Mika agreed, overhearing their conversation. Tonkawa was still conferring with the older and more experienced traders. "But how many beaches do you think there are in Mongollon?"

Tonkawa finished looking at the map. He folded it carefully on his knee and tucked it back into his pocket. The sun was three fingers short of midday.

"I found a trail that shouldn't be too bad," he said, looking up at them. "Gather your things now and give your thanks to your hosts." He got up himself and walked to the headman's house to retrieve his own pack.

The little Cahuilla girl cried when Child picked up her pack. Child bent to give her a hug. "Maybe I'll pass this way again on my way home," she said. She signed "thank you" to the man and woman who had shared their hut and their food. Then she went out to take her place on the traders' line.

"I'm glad we added more skins to these boots," Coyote said as they started off. "I thought I knew what cold felt like until I went outside this morning without them."

They wore their furs under their capes for warmth. The air around them got colder. Child kept her hands under her cape to hold it closed in the wind that blew the snow around them from the ground as they covered the high places of the trail. They sank to midcalf in the snow. Child felt it through her leggings. She began to wonder if she'd ever be warm again.

The several days' rest they had at the Cahuilla village refreshed them, and their pace helped to warm them. After a few days, the path began to descend, and soon, they were in the desert. Tonkawa told them that now the going would be easier. The worst was behind them.

They raised a small tent before it grew dark. The wind was still howling around them. They had to turn the tents skins-inward at the bottom and bolster them with their packs to keep them from flying away. Whenever they stopped, Child felt the cold more keenly.

The first time she saw Tonkawa's copper pot, she marveled. He had put snow and dried leaves in it and placed it directly in the fire. She had stared.

"It's metal," he explained. "It won't burn and it will melt the snow for our tea faster than a basket with firestones. You haven't seen baked clay pots yet. We make wonderful ones, but they break, so we don't bring them on trading journeys. The only trouble with copper is that it's so hard to extract from stone. Our people don't do it at all; the Olmecs and the Toltecs do. Probably metal will never take the place of pottery in our cities." He had sighed then.

111

No matter how many times she saw Tonkawa make tea in the marvelous copper pot, she continued to be impressed.

"They know so much, these city dwellers," she whispered to Coyote in Hokan that night. "There's so much we can learn from them."

"One thing makes me think most highly of Tonkawa," her friend replied thoughtfully. "He made you his daughter for as long as you remain with him."

"He calls all the men his sons even though only Sando and Okala are really his. In the pocheta brotherhood, a wot is like a father to all the people he leads."

"That may be true," Coyote agreed, "but in your case, he did it for your protection as well. It makes you a sister to every man here but me. How many young women would be safe sleeping in a tent with eight men who were not related to them?"

Child had not thought of that at all, but now she followed his thought at once. It increased the esteem she felt for Tonkawa.

"Thank you for explaining it to me, Uncle." She smiled to him. Before he pulled his furs over his head to sleep, she saw his answering grin by the glow of the fire coals.

Child lost track of the days. Three full moons had passed since they left Momoy's valley. There were signs now of spring coming. The snow was beginning to melt. Sometimes, they saw ground squirrels hurrying back and forth preparing their underground nests for their litters. The air smelled different. Even the birds began to sound happier when they sang their wake-up songs.

Child saw the cacti of her vision, with birds' nests

112

tucked in where their arms branched out. Tonkawa told Child and Coyote this was Mojave land, named after the people who lived here.

The men told her stories about these people. Some of the stories she was sure were only tales. She had difficulty taking Sando seriously when he told her the villagers collected caterpillars and fly larvae from the ponds to dry and grind for their flour.

Sando told her they thought their bread was delicious, as were the lizards they roasted. She could well believe that villages here must be poor. She would never wish to live where there were so few trees. At least there were a few streams Tonkawa knew about. She supposed there must be fish sometimes.

No civilized village turned pochetas away, but more likely than not, there was little enough food for the villagers themselves at this time of year.

In the distance, they saw a group of women with baskets beside them, digging. One of the women waved, motioning to them to come closer.

"A group of men traveling with a woman is not likely to be warlike, so they know we won't harm them," Okala observed. "It's good that you're with us, Sister."

The women's baskets contained roots and the green shoots of new-growing things. The woman who waved to them seemed to be in charge. She invited them to spend the night in her village.

As soon as they began to walk, Child saw the woman's eyes on the big bow she carried over her shoulder. It *was* bigger than most, and except for Coyote's, it was the biggest and strongest of all.

Before they reached the village, the woman was already trying in the sign language to bargain with Child for it. Child put a hand to her bow and shook her head vehemently. "Never," she said. "Momoy gave it to me."

"Their hunters use spears," Tonkawa told her as they walked. "They've seen our bows before, but none of them are as good as yours and Coyote's."

"We need them to hunt," the girl said. "I only hope I see something to shoot at before long."

"I'm sure you will," he said. "I saw some rabbits. You were looking the other way."

It was good to have a day to rest again. It was not very far now to Hohokam territory, but the weeks of walking through snow and the early spring rains were tiring.

The Mojaves insisted on sharing their food with the travelers. Now that the weather was warmer, they made their cooking fire outside, and everyone gathered around it. A few of the children came up hesitantly to Child. With her hair and her bow, she felt she was an oddity wherever she went. She was glad she had a chance to put her necklace inside her shirt before the villagers came close enough to see it.

The traders gave the last of their smoked meat to their hosts. They still had some cornmeal left. To Child, the villagers looked like walking bones with a layer of skin to keep it all together. The children were so thin, they made Coyote look fat in comparison, even now.

She wished they had more to give to them. The Month when Children Cry from Hunger was not long past. Child wondered how many of the village's children died during the harsh winter.

The traders were handed a basket containing some kind of bread. "But they have so little themselves," she protested, wondering also what it was made from.

"To refuse would be an insult," Tonkawa said. "Take some." They all took a bit. Child ate hers with suspicion. Tonkawa continued to explain. "These people take pride that they can survive here. They won't change their ways. That's why they continue to make spears when we would have shown them how to make arrows and bows."

"That woman seemed awfully interested in my bow if that's the case," Child observed. "Perhaps she has better sense than the rest of them. They ought to make her their wot. If we can walk from the ocean to the desert, they can walk to the forest for game and wood for bows and for pine nuts."

She had been thinking about the nuts Momoy gave her when she left. They were tucked in their pouch inside her shirt above her belt. She reached for them now and poured a handful of them into her hand.

She gathered the children close to her. It distressed her to see them so thin. She cracked one nut between her back teeth and threw the shells into the fire. The small nut meat was white and smooth. She looked at it for a moment, then popped it into her mouth and chewed it slowly. It was sweet and oily. It would be so good for these children. She only wished there were more of them. She shared them out evenly among the boys and girls. She was hungry herself, but she felt delight in the smiles of the children as they tasted the sweet nuts.

The men and the women of the village saw what she was doing. The woman who wanted Child's bow came over to her, more shyly now, to thank Child in her own language and with signs for feeding the children.

"Tomorrow, Coyote," she called across the fire, "we teach the Mojave how the Chumash hunt rabbits."

In the morning, Coyote and Child scouted the area

115

for rabbits. They found a large clump of prickly pear cacti. The same kind grew in their own land. Later in the year, the Mojave would have fruit to eat. There were only buds on them now where the flowers would grow. Often, these cacti provided hiding for snakes and small animals.

"A coyote wouldn't get a rabbit out from under this." Coyote pointed to the thorns.

"You should know. Do you see any rabbit spoor?"

"I think so. There are still some prints where the snow hasn't melted yet, but it's hard to say how old they are. I see some nibbled roots. Listen."

They held very still. Little sounds greeted their ears.

"I'll get the children and the stones," Child directed. "You get the hunters with their spears."

That night, both the villagers and the traders sat around their evening fire well content and munching on roasted rabbit.

"You make our way easier wherever we go," one of the men complimented Child. "I won't enjoy my next trip this well."

"Soon, Tupnek," Tonkawa promised, "soon you'll see a city."

CHAPTER 14

They followed the course of a river.
It was wide and rushing now with
the runoff of the melting snow. The
earth itself began to look different.
The sandstone of the cliffs and the
escarpments took on an orange
tone. They passed red rock canyons
and juniper-covered hillsides. They
kept the river within sight, but Tonkawa warned them not to get too
close to it. He told them that a
cloudburst in the mountains could
cause a flash flood here that could
sweep them all away.

Child looked suspiciously toward the mountains to check if
thunderclouds were lurking there.
They were not. The water was
somewhat salty here. It was called
the Salt River, although it was not
impossible to drink from because

of all the snow melt. But they filled their water bottles at springs when they could.

The river flowed into another, called the Gila. Then, close to the shade of a high red cliff, was a city! "This is not our home, Tupnek," Tonkawa hurried to explain. "This is a city of the Hohokam."

Coyote looked at the fields and the stone houses calmly. Child tried her best to follow his example in spite of the excitement she felt.

The city had many stone houses. Men worked in cultivated fields that made Momoy's garden look tiny in comparison. As much as Child wanted to see it all, she could tell right away that it was not the city her spirit guide called her to. Several small dogs ran up to bark at the strangers.

A party of men walked up to the traders where they waited at the outskirts of the city. One of the men, the only one who had his hair cut into a bang in the front as the traders did, detached himself from the group as soon as he saw Tonkawa.

The other men left. It was enough for them that the newcomers came in peace. The man who remained was about Tonkawa's age, but he was much bulkier. He looked well fed. He walked through the group, recognizing this trader and that one, saying their names and touching their hands in welcome.

He stopped in front of Tonkawa. "Tonkawa, my old friend!" his voice boomed. "You're on your way home loaded with treasure. What is this?" He saw Child. "You have a girl in your group. And who is this? He doesn't look like a Mongollon."

Tonkawa walked beside him until they stood beside Child and Coyote. "These are a couple of Chumash

118

friends who joined our expedition in Momoy's valley.
The young man is Coyote, her son, and the maiden is
her granddaughter, Tupnek."

"Children," he said to the two, "this is a pocheta. My
brother, and companion on many trips, Kataknek."

Child and Coyote bowed their heads to acknowledge
the introduction. I don't believe, Child thought to herself, that Kataknek travels anymore or carries heavy loads
now. She also decided that they were brothers by way
of the pocheta brotherhood, but not in fact. Their ac-
cents and their features were too different.

"I invite you to rest here," Kataknek said. "The men
can go to the pochetas' kiva for a sweat bath. You know
where it is, Tonkawa. I'll join you in a little while. My
wife will make arrangements for the girl. With your permission, Tonkawa?"

The trader nodded. Kataknek offered his arm in invitation. Child took it. As he walked her toward one of the
stone houses, she said, "I'm really glad you speak the
same language as the Mongollons here in the Hohokam
country."

A big smile came over the Hohokam's round face.
"You misunderstand. Very few of our people speak the
Mongollon language. I learned Tonkawa's and he learned
mine when we traded together as apprentices many years
ago. Come now and let me introduce you to my wife and
my children. Have you ever climbed a ladder before?"

She did not even know what a ladder was. A log
with notches in it was leaning against his house. Narrow
stones lying side by side and piled one on the other
made the walls. She did as he did, mounting the ladder
and descending to the interior of a round room. Part of
the house was underground. Near the ceiling, rectangu-

lar holes in the walls allowed light to enter and smoke to leave.

A stout woman, dressed in the smooth, light fabric of the traders, which they called cotton, watched them descend. She walked up to them. She wore a necklace of the summer-sky blue stones they called turquoise. Several of the children came to welcome their father and see who he had with him.

His words sounded like gibberish to her, exactly as the traders' language had before she began to learn it. Then he turned to her. "I told my wife you are a guest, a friend of a brother pocheta from Mongollon, who will be staying with her for a few days. I told her you're from the Far West Country."

"But, can't I stay with the traders? Where will you be? I can't speak here." Child's concern and worry showed in her voice.

He tried to calm her. "I'll be back to see how you're getting along when I come for dinner later. Only men may go into the kivas, except in very special circumstances. Humor my wife. Her name is Anasi. She'll prepare a bath for you. I see she's already looking at your hair. Just go along with her, Tupnek. She won't hurt you."

He turned and climbed out of the house before she could protest again.

Child stood very still while Anasi walked around her, mumbling in Hohokam either to Child or to her children, or possibly to herself. Child could not tell if the woman was expressing disapproval about her hair, or about her clothes, which were full of travel stains: sweat, and blood from animals she had butchered for food.

Did Anasi think she had time to wash her clothes and

120

put them out to dry? Child began to resent the inspection; then Anasi went into action. Watertight baskets were quickly filled. From the fire pit, Anasi took red-hot stones with tongs and dropped them into the water to warm it.

She gestured for Child to remove her garments. She set her girls to wetting and pounding yucca root and rubbing it into Child's clothes after they had been dampened.

While her girls worked on the clothing, Anasi handed a piece of sudsy yucca root to Child, who lathered herself with the slippery root. Anasi soaped her back. Then, she rinsed Child with cotton cloths dipped in the hot water and wrung out. She dried Child and wrapped her in a cotton robe.

She helped Child unbraid her long hair. With a beautiful comb fashioned from a pink shell, she started working on one side. An older daughter with a plain wooden comb worked at untangling and brushing out the other side.

Child had never felt this pampered in all her life. She ignored the little pulls as the two worked. She stretched with pleasure inside the loose cotton robe. They soaped up her hair, working the lather from the ends down to her scalp until the top of her head tingled.

One of the girls led her up the ladder to a second ladder, which led to the roof. Another handed up clay pots sloshing over with tepid water.

They had Child lie down with her head at the edge of the roof so her hair could hang down. They poured water over her hair, washing away the suds until her hair was squeaky clean and shining. She needed help to squeeze out all the water.

On the roof were drying racks. Child assumed they were for tobacco or meat, but they were empty now and they looked clean. One of the boys climbed up carrying Child's now-clean garments to lay them out to dry in the sun along with all the washing cloths and even some of the family's clothes. She had seen cotton cloth before, but never in as many colors as this.

While Child sat on the roof in the warm, late-spring sunshine, waiting for her hair to dry, Anasi came to sit beside her. The older woman knew only a little of the sign language. She tried to ask where Child came from. At least, it seemed so.

Child told her "Far, very far away. From mountains near the great water, as far as anyone can see." Being the wife of a trader, Anasi must have heard of the ocean, but, Child imagined, it was the way she, herself, had heard of the three levels of the world. Except for the level they lived on, they were places of legend. One did not expect for someone to arrive from there. Anasi put her hand to her cheek and shook her head slowly.

At last, she turned to more practical things. Her son and daughters helped her bring her small, flat-topped cooking stove up to the roof. The boy went down and came up again. He poured hot coals from a wide-mouthed clay jar into the bottom of it.

Clay pots were as unbelievable to Child as the ocean must have been to Anasi. She determined to learn how they were made. Perhaps her own people could make use of them. She doubted, though, that they would ever replace the accustomed cooking baskets. Baskets were lighter and they seldom broke, but they could not sit right in the fire pits the way clay pottery could. The metal cooking pot was even more convenient, now that

she could compare, but as Tonkawa said, metal was un-
likely to replace clay pots. People liked best what they
were used to.

She wondered if the desert people were ever going
to put away their spears and darts and atlatls to use bows
and arrows the way more advanced people did to bring
down their food. It was hard to change.

While the stew cooked over the fire pit, Anasi made
her bread on the roof. She took a bowl of fine cornmeal.
Child recognized it by now. She mixed it with water into
a loose batter and cooked flat cakes of it very quickly,
piling them into a basket until the batter was gone.

They watched the sun begin to set over the red hills.
Anasi decided it was time to go back inside. Before Kataknek returned, Child's hair had been gathered into two
coils, one over each ear. She was dressed by Anasi and
her two oldest daughters in a black dress with blue trim.
Her left shoulder was bare. The cloth of dress went over
her right shoulder. Around her waist was tied a leather
belt with tubes of turquoise hanging on the thongs. She
wore her jade-and-gold necklace proudly, a symbol of
her connection to Tonkawa.

Kataknek moved across the room to look at her. "I
see my wife made you into a proper young lady," he
said, nodding appreciatively. Child did not know herself
when one of the girls held up an iron pyrite mirror for
her to look in after Anasi was through dressing her and
arranging her hair.

More men came down the ladder now. Tonkawa was
first. Then Sando and Okala descended the ladder. The
three of them stood back to look at her. Coyote arrived
last. He got off the ladder and looked around, letting his
eyes grow accustomed to the dim light. He wore a cotton

kilt like the others. He kept looking, as though he expected something to be seen there; he looked first at the younger children, then at the two oldest girls and Child. Not a flicker of recognition crossed his face. At last, he looked to Kataknek's wife.

"What did your wife do with my friend?" he asked almost angrily in Mongollon of their host. "Tonkawa told me she was here. I promised to protect her."

Child suppressed a giggle. "I'm right here, Coyote," she said. She gestured with her hands to the dress and her hair. "*This* is what she did to me. What do you think?"

Coyote blinked and looked at her again. "By all the stars and spirits," he swore in Hokan, "you really *are* a woman."

The next morning, Kataknek walked through the city and the fields with Child and Coyote. Most of the houses were like Anasi's. "The women own all the houses in our cities," Kataknek told them. "It's the same with Tonkawa's people and the cities up north. The women own the fields too."

"What do the men own?" Child asked. It seemed like an upside-down world.

"We own the crops until they are harvested. The kivas also belong to the men. They are the deep, wide pit houses. We have our ceremonies there and sleep there. We have our sweat baths in the kivas and smoke the sacred tobacco. Except in very special circumstances, no women are allowed to go into the kivas.

"Do you see this cloth that we wear? The cotton it is made of belongs to us. Look." He brought them down a row of cotton plants. "When the buds open, there will be flowers. Then the flowers will turn into white, soft fluff, almost as soft as rabbit fur. In the kivas, the men

124

spin the cotton fluff into yarn, and then we weave it into cloth. We make the clothes into these beautiful colors you see our women wearing. It is a man's skill like cooking is a woman's.

"Look." He pointed. "There is one of my girls walking with Tonkawa's son. What is his name?"

"Okala," Coyote answered. "He's looking for a wife." Child wondered if she heard a bit of spite in his voice or if she imagined it.

"I can't ask for a better son-in-law than a son of Tonkawa's," Kataknek said firmly. "He'll only be home long enough to give my daughter children, but never long enough to make her tired of him. The wife of a trader is a lucky woman. They'll make their home here of course, so Tania can stay with her mother's people."

He raised his arm to the young couple and they returned his wave. "Now you've already seen our ball-playing field. I can show you our dam and our irrigating canals. We invented them, you know, and they're the best in the world."

He led them to the raised mounds of earth lined with rock and showed them where a wooden lock could be raised to allow water from the Gila River to come and flood the farmland. They climbed up a slope to look down at a rectangle of water. It struck Child that these people had actually changed the course of a river. Such intelligence, such use of special techniques to make food grow, gave her a feeling of being very small.

"How do you make your clay pottery? What is clay?" she asked.

"It is found by the riverbank. It's a special kind of earth that holds together so it can be shaped. It gets hard when it's baked in a very hot fire. The women work the

125

clay. Your friends, the Mongollons, learned how to make pottery first. They taught us. With different kinds of clay, we make different color pots. Our women make beautiful patterns to paint on the jars and pots before they're baked. The Mongollons even taught the Northern People. They got tired of trading their baskets for them. We used to call them the Basket Makers, but ever since their emissaries came to the Mongollons to learn, they make some of the best pottery in the world."

"Can you show me clay? Can you show me how to work it?" Child did not try to cover the excitement in her voice. Here was something new to learn!

They climbed down to the Gila River. It was shallow now, moving slowly. She could easily have waded to the other side, she decided, without getting wet past her middle. Some of the women were there on the banks, digging for clay. Anasi was there with them. She saw her husband bringing Coyote and Child, and motioned for them to come closer.

Child became so engrossed in learning about clay and the woman in showing her that they did not notice when Kataknek and Coyote walked away. They almost did not hear the distant thunder in the mountains; it was so far away. Child looked up. The sun was still shining. Then she heard the rumble of the river. There was a splash and one of the women shrieked.

Child followed with her eyes to where the woman pointed frantically. Her child had fallen on the slippery clay and tumbled over the embankment. The river, so quiet a short time ago, had become suddenly high with the runoff from the storm over the mountains.

The boy's mother was held by the others and pulled back from the now-raging water. She screamed hysterically again and again for help, beating with her hands against the others, who were holding her back.

They tried to tell her that it was too late. They tried to comfort her. Child did not see how it could be too late. She ran along the embankment. The boy's head was above the surface of the water. She did not see the men from the fields who rushed up to try to stop her. She pushed past them until she was ahead of the child at a point higher than the water. Then she ran to the land's edge and jumped.

She tried to ignore the iciness of the water. It was a battle to get where she could grab the young boy. She tried to call to him, but the sound of the water drowned her voice. If only it was not too late, as all the people seemed to think.

He was swept in front of her. She reached out and grabbed him. There was no sign of life in the small form, but she still tucked him under one arm so she could hold his head above the water. She pulled hard with her other arm and kicked for shore. At last, she felt gravel under her feet.

She barely had the strength to pull him all the way out of the water. She lay on the bank, gasping for breath, when the townspeople reached them.

"The boy is dead," she heard Tonkawa say to her in Mongollon. "Give him to his mother and father to mourn for."

She understood his words, but she did not believe it.

"No!" she shouted. She felt so heavy and weak herself, she could hardly move. The cold water had taken almost all her strength. She thought she felt some warmth returning to the little boy when she was carrying him. She was not ready to give up yet.

She turned him over onto his stomach with his head facing downhill and pressed with both hands on his back. She released the pressure and did it again several times. He coughed and trembled. She repeated the motion until water began to run out of his mouth and nose. He coughed and gasped again. Then he sat up and began to cry for his mother.

Now, Child could see Coyote keeping the people back so they could not interfere. The young mother must have been beside herself with grief, not knowing what this stranger was doing to her son's body. Child was doing what she had been taught to do in Wene'mu to try to save someone from drowning, but the poor woman could not have known that.

As soon as the boy sat up, Coyote moved aside. The mother rushed to gather her son into her arms. After a moment, the boy's father lifted him and carried him over to where Child sat, soaking wet and shivering, to thank her before they took him home.

Tonkawa lifted Child to carry her back to the city. Her skin was like ice. Coyote ran ahead to find a blanket. "How did you know what to do?" he asked her. "How did you learn how to swim like that?"

In a flash of insight, she realized that desert people would never have learned to swim. It was a skill she took for granted as much as walking. She felt herself begin to slip into unconsciousness. A cold wind was blowing. She understood that Coyote was trying to keep her from falling asleep and that it would be dangerous to do so.

"Well," she said slowly, "I spent half of my life swimming in the ocean. I should hope I can swim in a river." Then everything went dark.

CHAPTER 15

During the next few days, Child slipped in and out of consciousness. She was aware of feeling warm, too warm, in fact. She kicked off a covering that was so light, there was no way it could be giving off so much heat. Cool, damp cloths were placed on her forehead and hands. She remembered Coyote watching over her, worry and concern showing through his dark eyes. He seemed almost afraid to touch her, as though he were worried that she might dissolve.

She saw Anasi bending over her and the children running here and there at their mother's direction. Was she in Anasi's house, then? She did not remember how she got there. Anasi tried to spoon broth into her mouth, but she could not swallow. She had no desire for food.

Then she was in another house, deeper and darker. Torches burned around the large circular room. Tonkawa and all her brothers were around her. She was lying on the floor. An imposing man she never saw before was making beautiful pictures around her where she lay, by pouring different colored sands out of small-necked clay jars. She seemed to see him from above as if she were floating.

He was making geometrically stylized pictures of the sun, of clouds in a turquoise sky, and of birds flying. It was so pretty, she wished she could fly up to touch the birds. The largest of them looked like the condor she had seen in her vision, who told her to fly east to visit the cities.

She felt then as though she were falling up, into the turquoise-colored sky. "There you are," said the great bird. His wings were outstretched the way they had been when she first saw him above Momoy's valley. "The old man is still waiting for you. You must hurry and get well."

"Am I sick?" Child asked.

"You are very sick," the bird answered, watching her through his hooded eyes. "That's why you're in the men's kiva. You saved the sun priest's grandson. Did you know that?"

"No. I only know I saved a little boy. That's all. I didn't care who he was."

The bird nodded. "It's a blessing from the Mother that you were here when you were needed."

His praise made her glow with pleasure, and she

smiled. From far below them, she heard men's voices growing excited.

"How will I find the old man?" she asked. She was afraid she did not have much more time to speak with the bird.

"Go north, to the largest city of the Northern People. On a flat-topped hill near it, you will see a round tower that is sacred to the sun. When you see me on the tower, you will know that the old man is waiting for you within. Get well now and hurry to him."

"I will," she promised, and sat up.

As she did, the chanting around her stopped. Coyote was close by. He looked up and opened his mouth silently in a private prayer of thanksgiving. The imposing man rubbed away the sand picture immediately. Then he spoke to her. Tonkawa hurried forward to translate.

"He says Sun Father and Earth Mother gave you back to us. He wants to know what made you smile."

"I smiled when the great condor praised me for saving the boy."

"The Great Condor?" It was the sun chief repeating Tonkawa's words. She saw his robe now, painted with the sun and its rays. He spoke to her again.

Tonkawa translated. "He says the Great Condor is a spirit who only speaks to chiefs and holy men."

"I don't know about that," Child answered. She felt confused. "Maybe it was only a regular condor. I saw him during my spirit vision when I was in Momoy's valley. He told me to come to the cities to look for an old man who needs help. I have to hurry. Can someone lead me to the biggest city of the Northern People?

The sun chief looked at her as if he were seeing a

vision himself. He closed his eyes and mumbled to himself. He held his hands out flat over the earth of the kiva and listened. After a bit, he nodded. He spoke to the other chiefs and then to Tonkawa and Kataknek.

Tonkawa spoke to Child now, in Mongollon mixed with sign to be sure she understood well. "It's time for my sons and me to finish our journey home. Now that you're well again, Kataknek and the sun chief along with a guard of honor will bring you to the holy Half-Sun City. He knows which one you mean. We'll take you back to Anasi's house now. In the morning, we must take our leave of you. Tupnek, only Earth Mother knows how glad we are that we had you with us during our journey and how much we'll miss you."

She could not speak for the emotion she felt. Tonkawa lifted her into his arms to carry her back to her bed.

In the morning, Tonkawa and the Mongollon traders came to the house of Anasi to bid Child and Coyote farewell. Each of their "brothers" came up to embrace them. When it was Okala's turn, he had Kataknek and Anasi's daughter, his new bride, with him. They both looked joyous; Child felt their gladness. The girl said something in Hohokam and Okala translated.

"She said she hopes good fortune will accompany you wherever you go."

"Tell her I hope her mother-in-law likes her," Child answered. The girl laughed.

"Good fortune, Brave One," Sando said. "Don't walk into any tar pits on your way home." She tried to smile. The chances were she would never see any of them again.

Tonkawa embraced her last. "You are an honorary pocheta now. Never forget that."

"I won't," Child managed to say. Then she ran up to give him one last hug.

"I wish you were really my daughter," he whispered in her ear. Then, the traditional good-bye from one pocheta to another: "May Earth Mother guide your footsteps."

He embraced Coyote next. The young man looked as sorrowful as she felt. "May she guide your footsteps too, my son. I shall miss your flute and your appetite."

"I never had anyone who was like a father to me before, Tonkawa," Coyote said. "I won't forget you."

The traders formed their line with their heavy packs. The Hohokam woman walking beside Okala looked like a hummingbird beside mudhens.

The townspeople watched them walk east until they were almost out of sight. Then Coyote lifted his voice and let out a high, melodious yell. The traders turned to look back. Coyote and Child waved. Kataknek and Anasi waved to their daughter and to their new son-in-law. Then the line moved behind a hill, and they were gone.

"We'll leave when the sun is high," Kataknek told them.

Anasi gave them both beautiful new thick-soled moccasins for their journey. "I'll make you both another pair to walk home in," she signed after she handed the soft hide boots to them. She had been practicing the sign language. She laughed. It was fun to talk with hands. Child and Coyote thanked her.

"The trip," Kataknek told them as he helped them pack, "will take about twelve days. The highways will make traveling easier when we get to the Northern Peo-

133

ple's country, and we shouldn't have to worry about Marauders up there either. There will be soldiers watching from the guard towers."

"What did he mean by 'highways'?" Child asked Coyote when they had a chance to talk alone.

"I don't know," he answered. "What did he mean by 'Marauders' and 'guard towers' and 'soldiers'?"

This was more like a parade than an expedition. Child wondered why they made such a fuss. A quest in search of a spirit guide should have been more private, but she could not offend her hosts.

Kataknek walked with her and Coyote most of the time. With his Mongollon speech and signs, he was able to pass on whatever any of the others wanted to communicate to them.

"Do you speak the language of the Northern People?" Child asked him as they walked.

"Yes, and some of the sun priests do. Do you have sun priests in your home near the ocean?"

"Of course," she replied indignantly. "We honor all the gods, but Earth Mother especially. I was young when I left my two villages to go live with Grandmother Momoy, but I think we even have a high priest who's called an alchuklash. He's the one who reads the stars and tells the people what will be. Isn't that right, Coyote?"

The land became more barren and stark with fewer rivers and springs as they walked north. They sheltered in Hohokam cities the first few nights, but they were soon past Hohokam territory. High rock formations of oddly shaped red sandstone grew out of the land here. It was a strange place.

Another day of walking brought them close to what

134

Kataknek described as the Great Canyon. He brought them to see it after the night's camp was set up. "There's a river at the bottom. A few villages are down there. It's too far out of our way to visit them, but I want you to see the canyon. It is so huge, a man standing on one edge can't see or hear a man standing on the other. It will be something to tell your children about."

Child wondered how any canyon could be that big. Then, she saw it.

"You know," Coyote said, looking out at the vast panorama of multicolored rock cliffs, "no one will believe this, exactly the way people here don't believe in the ocean. It's a thing a person has to see for himself." He whistled. Far below, a pair of coyotes howled as if in answer.

"I have some cousins down there," he said wistfully.

"I wish we had more time to explore." Child put a hand on his shoulder to console him. "At least we saw it. *We* know we saw it. Come on, let's get back to our camp."

They saw a few members of the wandering bands Kataknek told them about. Sometimes they attacked travelers, he had told them. They made war for the joy of fighting and to take away what belonged to others.

The Marauders watched the travelers from the hills. Child saw that their faces were painted into frightening scare-masks. Travelers were not to be harmed where she came from. There were some who had no respect for the laws of civilized people. She decided that she was grateful for the extra company after all.

They came within sight of an imposing hill. On its peak stood a round stone structure. There were men on the hill watching them.

"Is that one of their cities?" Child asked. She was anticipating something bigger.

"No." Kataknek shaded his eyes to look into the distance. "It's one of their watchtowers. We'll be safe from Marauders now. We ought to see a highway as soon as we pass the tower rock."

The priests, who were walking in the front of the procession, waved their sun banners. A column of smoke began to rise from the tower.

"We'll be expected now," Kataknek explained. "Black smoke would have meant we were enemies. At night, they light fires. Each watchtower sends the signal to the next one."

Coyote shook his head when he saw the highway. "This is too much," he said. Ten people could have walked side by side on this broad roadway.

"Look here," Child said, running to the side of the wide road. There were small walls edging both sides.

"What other miracles can the Northern People perform?" Coyote demanded. "Do they grow food without water?"

Kataknek wiped his forehead and looked serious when Child expected him to smile. "It seems so sometimes. The Mongollon and the Hohokam have taught these people everything they know, but they keep their own secrets well. No more questions for now." He pulled a waterskin from his pack and drank. Walking and explaining were drying his mouth.

They passed great stone mountains with flat tops as they walked through the land. Aside from the cities they passed, there were other wonders. There were bridges made of stone and wood to cross the washes. There were stone steps cut into the very rock to help travelers ascend to the higher elevations. How organized the people must be who made them! Child thought.

The travelers spent several nights in the cities they passed through. These cities were even grander than those of the Hohokam people. There were still the circular pit kivas, but there were towers too. Child could hardly believe her eyes when she finally saw the multi-storied buildings of her datura vision. These, Kataknek said, were only the outliers, not the main cities.

In the cities where they were given shelter for the night, turkeys wandered through the streets. The city dwellers needed planks in front of their doorways to keep the dirty, noisy birds out.

The people they encountered were polite, if not friendly. Child was surprised that thirty men and a woman were so easily accommodated. Whenever the Hohokam travelers approached one of the cities, the priests raised their sun banners and other priests came to greet them. The men were brought to the sun kiva or the traders' kiva.

Child had to be taken to some woman's house, where she tried her best to get along without speaking the language. If only everyone spoke the same way, she thought, things would be so much easier. At least there was the sign language, but not everyone bothered to learn it. The woman of the house gave her a turkey egg omelet to eat with flat corn bread piki for breakfast. The turkey meat the night before was simmered with squash and onions until it could be eaten almost without chewing.

Child thanked her hostess for her hospitality. The

woman wanted to know where Child's people came from. She had never seen a young woman dressed in a tunic and leggings before.

Child's sign motions, which indicated very much water to the west, so wide that it could not be crossed, made her hostess smile and sign, "You don't have to tell me if you don't want to."

When they formed their traveling line, Kataknek said, "We're almost to Half-Sun City now. We'll pass their sun house by midday." Child caught Coyote's look.

It was late afternoon when they approached the white stone sun temple on the hill. Below, not very far from a dry, sunbaked arroyo, was Half-Sun City. Child looked down at it and felt herself shiver. "Can it really be?" she whispered. "It's the city of my vision, Coyote. Will he be here?"

Coyote took her arm and pointed at the sky. A bird with wide, outspread wings wheeled in great circles as it descended from a cloud. All the priests stared at it as if they were hypnotized, shading their eyes from the sun. The closer the bird came, the larger it appeared to be. Riding a wind current, barely moving its wings, it made for the roof of the sun house. When it reached the roof, it landed and folded its great wings.

"Do you see it too?" Child asked Coyote.

"I see it. Everyone sees it. All the priests are staring so hard, it's as if they've turned to stone." He pushed Kataknek. The man did not move. "What's the matter with you?" He turned to Child. "What's the matter with all of them?" he demanded.

"I don't know," Child whispered. "Shh. The bird is talking to me." Coyote looked from her to the bird, confused. After a while, Child nodded. "Coyote, I have to go inside." She squeezed his hand. "Don't be afraid. It will be all right, I think. Wait for me here." She walked toward the doorway without looking back.

"I'll wait," he said.

CHAPTER 16

It was dark inside the sun's house, except for a narrow rectangle of sunlight high on the wall opposite where Child stood. Her eyes became accustomed gradually to the dimness. She walked forward to look at the room.

There were two descending ramps, one on each side of a raised fire pit. There was no fire burning now. The shadow of the room was chilling after her long climb in the afternoon sun.

"Where are you?" she called. In the small, quiet room her voice sounded louder than it should have.

An old man with white hair flowing down his shoulders climbed one of the ramps and walked toward her. Beneath his broad forehead, intelligent eyes searched her face. "At last you have come," he said.

She watched him closely, trying to tell if he was someone she may have known before. She could not remember his face, but somehow he seemed familiar to her. She realized quite suddenly that he answered her in the same language that she used, Hokan, the language of her birth.

He held his hands out to her in invitation. As soon as she took them, she felt a completeness. He was the one she walked half a year to find.

"Who are you?" she asked.

"I am as you see me. I am only an old man who wishes to go home. I'm needed there. You must be the deliverer my spirit bird sent to me."

"Your name is Old Man?"

He bowed his head. Then he raised his eyes to hers.

"Your name?" he asked.

"Tupnek."

"Why do you call yourself a child when you are a full-grown woman?"

At his words, she covered her eyes. Tears of elation filled them. After a while, she wiped her cheeks with the back of one hand and looked at him again.

"My name is not Tupnek any more. It's New Woman now that I've found you, as you told me it would be. I have been walking for half a year with my friend Coyote and some traders. Priests from the Hohokam country brought me here. Why can't you go home, Old Man?"

He guided her to the stone ledge of the cold, raised fire pit, where they could be comfortable.

"Sit beside me, New Woman, and I'll tell you. I once was what is called in the land of our people an al-chuklash.

"I was able to look into the stars and into my dreams for visions of the future, of things that would come to be. I was expected by the wot of my village to give advice to guide him and his people.

"Sometimes, though, my visions were not as clear as they might have been. It will be fourteen years next winter solstice since I made a prediction that did not come true.

"I saw a youth in the dream I had. He was dressed in leggings and a tunic as you wear now, and his hair was cut across the forehead as yours is. He was far from his people on a quest, but when I awoke from my vision, I knew that he was destined to become one of the greatest leaders the Chumash people have ever known. When he grew up, he was to unite three warring villages in peace, the village of his father, one near the shore, and one in a hidden valley.

"Perhaps even then I was too old to interpret my vision properly. I had already seen forty summers. My hair was nearly as white as you see it now and I was already called Old Man. I was sure my dream spoke the truth. Perhaps I should not have opened my mouth and told what I saw.

"Instead of this wonderful boy the wot of my village was waiting for, a girl was born. In any case, the wot divorced his good wife and disowned his daughter. On that day, he told me to leave and never come back.

"I wandered for years, traveling and living here and there. I must have predicted a few things correctly because the high sun priest here in Half-Sun City invited me to stay. The problem is that now I feel I must return to the mountains that were once my home. My dreams tell me there will be a terrible famine. The Mother is angry and she will keep the rains from coming. If I do not return to give warning and help, many people will die. This is why I was praying for a deliverer. The sun priest does not give me permission to leave."

During his long story, he spoke with his eyes on the strong ponderosa pine beams that held up the adobe bricks of the roof. He did not see that the young woman sitting beside him held her hands over her eyes again; so intent was he on telling the tale. When he finished, he turned to her.

"New Woman! I know my story is a sad one, but it won't help to cry. New Woman!" He stood up and put his hands on her shoulders, trying to comfort her.

Finally, she was able to compose herself. "Old Man," she said. "Listen to me." Her voice, which was hardly above a whisper when she began, strengthened as she spoke.

"I was born on the day of winter solstice. When it comes again, I will have seen fourteen summers. I was born in the village of Sa'aqtik'oy. My mother's name is Pretty One from the village of Wene'mu by the ocean. My father, although he won't acknowledge it, is Sword-fish. Do you *now* know who I am?"

She appeared to grow before his eyes as she spoke. She stood and he saw her rise as a star rises. He saw, once again, the solstice pole with its crown of feathers bursting into flame. He saw how it was extinguished moments later by the downpour, while lightning and thunder played across the dark skies above the mountains. Everyone muttered, "Mother's blessing" when it

143

happened. It was the sign of tragedy averted through the goodness of the Mother, but no one understood then what the tragedy was. In the events that followed, it might even have been forgotten. At last, he understood. She stood before him.

"I know who you are," he said softly. "My mistaken understanding of my dream caused you and your mother pain and sorrow. Will you ever be able to forgive me?"

"But don't you see, Old Man? If you had not misread what you saw, we would not be here at all. We wouldn't have learned what we need to save our people: corn and irrigation. It can get our people, my three villages, through the drought!"

"The Mother works in mysterious ways," Old Man said in wonder when it all became clear to him. "It's time to go home." He took her hand and guided her out into the sunlit plaza before the sun's house.

As soon as the pair emerged, the bird flew away and the magic was over. All the people looked in vain for the giant condor they thought they saw perched on its roof.

Coyote rushed to them. "Child. What happened? Is this the old man your spirit told you to find?"

"You must be Coyote," Old Man said. "I am. Apparently, your friend and I share the same spirit guide. Her name is no longer Tupnek. It is New Woman now. We must hurry home, Coyote. We have much to accomplish there and very little time."

"But look!" Coyote pointed down. A great party of men were climbing up from the city to the sun's plaza.

The Hohokam priests tried to greet them, but they were pushed, not too gently, out of the way.

The high sun priest, if his elaborate robe and head-dress were any indication, walked directly up to the

144

Hohokam sun priest and began to question him. Anger was the only part of his speech that New Woman was able to understand.

Kataknek tried to come forward to explain what was being said in the confrontation, but he was held back.

Old Man, his hand still tightly holding New Woman's, walked up to the two men and spoke to them both. Then he turned to New Woman.

"He is demanding to know why your friends came to the holiest shrine of the sun without asking for his permission first. He also wants to know how you dared to speak to 'his' holy man."

He directed his translation to New Woman, not to the Hohokam sun priest. He was already acknowledging her as his wot. More than anything else could have, this gave her the confidence she needed.

She smiled when the high priest expected her to cower. She motioned for Coyote to come to Old Man's other side.

"Translate, please, Old Man," she directed. Then she faced the sun priest and spoke to him directly, waiting while Old Man translated her words for the northern priest.

"We three are Chumash. We come from the land to the far west, where the sun sets over the wide water. We are going home."

The sun priest appeared almost to back down, to stand aside and let them pass. Then he realized what he was doing and stopped.

"No." The sound was emphatic enough for New Woman to understand without waiting for translation.

Coyote turned toward his old friend now. "Perhaps we can make a bargain for him. I have some of Momoy's powdered roots here in my pack. Shall we see how much they're worth to this priest?"

"Go ahead and try." She squeezed his hand. "Good luck."

With Old Man translating, Coyote explained about the magic vision powders. New Woman watched the priest's face grow interested as he listened.

"He wants to test it," Old Man translated to both of them. But that would take time.

"His request is fair," New Woman reluctantly agreed. "Coyote, take him to his kiva and show him how the powder is used. We will be waiting here. Old Man, tell him we will wait two days only, but we must have food and water brought to us. Tell him the sun will be watching to see if his high priest is an honorable man who keeps his word."

Coyote and half the priests, along with Kataknek who Coyote insisted must come to translate, began to climb down toward the village. New Woman saw from the high place where they stood that the white stone Half-Sun City was still growing. There were very few cultivated fields nearby and no river. The wash was dry. Maybe Old Man could explain.

Before she could ask, he spoke to her. "No one ever talked that way to the high sun priest before," he said.

"Then, it's time someone did," she replied tartly.

It was past midday, two days later, when the chief priest, followed by many men and led by Coyote on one side and Kataknek on the other, climbed once more to the plaza. He walked up to New Woman more respectfully this time and he allowed Kataknek to walk with him. Coyote came to stand beside New Woman and the old holy man.

Old Man asked the priest something. He replied with obvious arrogance and then asked a question of his own. When they finished speaking, New Woman looked to Old Man for an explanation.

"He dreamed of mice. He does not want my help to interpret the meaning of his vision. He is a high priest. He thinks it would be beneath his dignity to ask for my help. But he liked Momoy's powders. He said he wants to deal regularly with Kataknek's people for more of it."

"Good. So, he'll let Old Man leave with us."

"Not yet. He wants to know what else you'll give him."

New Woman bit back her reply. She turned to the others. "He knows how I value you, Old Man. That's the worst way to begin negotiations."

Old Man smiled. "I never expected to be held for ransom. If I had foreseen it, I wouldn't have made myself so useful."

"You can't help it, Old Man," Coyote said with a laugh. "That's why we need to get you home. New Woman, think very hard to Momoy. Maybe she'll give you an idea of what to offer this greedy priest. I'll help you."

New Woman pictured Momoy working in her garden. Help us, Grandmother, she thought. She explained the situation as well as she could. I don't know what will appease him, but we've got to get Old Man back. Then, she listened.

She heard no answer in her head. Coyote had done this before. Maybe he was having better luck. She opened her eyes and looked to him. He shrugged helplessly. Perhaps they were too far away.

New Woman could not think of a thing. The priest was grinning. The men from the Hohokam country and Coyote watched her intently to see what she was going to do. Old Man only shook his head. "Some leader I'm turning out to be," New Woman muttered in Hokan to him. "My first trial and I can't even make a deal for your release."

She felt the sun getting hot, shining down on the plaza. She could not think. The sweat on her neck began to itch unbearably. A buzzing fly settled on her neck. Without thinking, she scratched. The jade-and-gold necklace, put away beneath her tunic top and forgotten, fell and jangled on the stone. She bent to retrieve it.

The high priest pointed with a finger. He laughed. He almost danced with joy at discovering the treasure New Woman had been hiding.

"He says he'll take that for Old Man's freedom," Kataknek interpreted. "He says it shines like the sun and should belong to the high sun priest of Half-Sun City."

New Woman shook her head negatively. "I can't give that. Tonkawa gave it to me." Kataknek took her arm. He led her a few steps away. Then, he spoke to her in a whisper.

"Think, New Woman." He kept his voice to a whisper in case any of the northern priests or chiefs understood Mongollon. The sign language was too universal and they could be seen. "Think what Tonkawa said to you just before they left. I was close enough to overhear."

"He said he wished I really *was* his daughter. That's why I can't part with this." She fingered the necklace. Tears began to fill her eyes again. She was afraid of losing

148

all her composure and with it Old Man's chance for freedom.

"I didn't hear *that*. That was not what I was referring to. Of course, he would. A man would have to be a fool not to. No," he said, "I meant when he said you are an honorary pocheta. Remember everything he taught you about trading. I'm sure he must have told you a thing is valuable because of its use or for what you can get for it. Would you remember Tonkawa without a pretty necklace, one that you are afraid to allow to be seen anyway?"

"Of course I would."

"Then make a good trade, and make Tonkawa proud of you."

New Woman took a deep breath. They walked back to the sun priest. "This necklace is valuable," she told him, giving Kataknek time to translate. "I would be very unhappy to give it up. Look at it again. Examine the stones and the workmanship. Pochetas traveled three years to bring it to me. Do you expect me to let it go for one old man?"

"What do you want, then?"

"I want three baskets of planting corn and the loan of three of your best farmers for the next planting season. I also want an armed escort to see me, this old man, and all my followers back to the Hohokam city. Do you agree?"

The sun priest consulted with the other men of rank who were standing nearby. Then he replied, "I agree."

It was almost enough. "We are in your power here in your country and your reach is wide," New Woman continued. She wanted a guarantee. She hoped it would not make him angry. "Before your sun, will you swear to keep my conditions? And not only before the sun who

149

sleeps during the night, but also before the earth who is always with us."

The sun priest took his oath twice, once facing the sky and once kneeling, with his hands touching the ground.

New Woman held the necklace up as if showing it to the sun. Real tears glittered in her eyes. Tonkawa's gift no longer belonged to her. She hoped he would hear about the deal she made for it and be proud of her. Then she handed it to the high sun priest. We did it, Grandmother, she thought. Thank you for reminding me of the necklace.

They were invited to partake of a meal in the city itself before they departed and to offer prayers for a safe journey while the corn seeds were collected and the three farmers were found.

There were fewer people in the city than New Woman would have guessed for such an enormous place. Coyote must have wondered also, for he questioned Old Man as they ate in the grand plaza. The terraced apartments rose around them like the crescent moon. The flat roofs of each level made the terraces for the level above. In the middle of the crescent, there were four stories. The sides were being added to.

"People come from all the cities around to ceremonies and dances during the holy solstice seasons," Old Man explained. "They come for the harvest celebrations and for other special events too. Only the workers, the builders, the priests, and their families live here all year round. It has to have this many rooms and kivas for all the holiday visitors. That is why you see so few gardens here. The visitors bring their own food and leave enough for the residents. Very few people die here either, in case you wondered why you didn't see any cemeteries."

"Now it makes sense," Coyote said. "It's hard to imagine so many people living together as this place would hold. I know I wouldn't like it."

"It's not where I would choose to live either," New Woman added, "although it must be very pretty with all the colored banners flying. They're already starting to put them up for summer solstice. I can almost imagine the dancers in their fine clothes with the pipes and drums playing and the rattles shaking. It's a shame we can't wait for it."

Three northern men, packs on their backs, walked up to them. Their families walked behind the men. Old Man rose to greet them.

"They are our planters," he explained. "Their wives and families have come to see them off. It will be several years before they see their husbands and fathers again."

"Oh. I never thought of that." Young Woman held her upper lip between her teeth, thinking. She needed the special skill these men possessed. If Earth Mother would allow them to reach home in time for the next spring planting, they could have enough corn to feed the people of Sa'aqtik'oy, of Wene'mu, and of Crab's village during the drought that was coming. The water in Momoy's spring should be enough for these three men who knew how to coax corn from the earth with very little water.

She knelt and put her hands on the ground. "Please, Earth Mother," she whispered softly, "allow us to plant corn, just this once, even though you never sent Corn Woman to my people. We'll send back any we don't

151

need. We'll never plant it again without your permission. Please."

Old Man heard her words. Unless Earth Mother allowed it, the corn would not grow. He added his own prayer.

New Woman began to rummage through her pack. "Coyote," she said, "let's give these people some of the perfect shells we brought. The pochetas said they value them here. We can give the rest to the Hohokam for their help."

The families made much over the shells. The high sun priest and the other priests came to bless them and wish them a good journey. He wore his new necklace over his yellow-and-blue robe. Stones last longer than people, New Woman thought to herself. How many more times would this same necklace change hands? How many more people would wear it?

Twenty more men took their places before and behind the departing travelers. They stood four across. No wonder the roads were so wide. So many people could use them at once.

Old Man took a last look at the house of the sun as they passed it. He laid one hand on the stones that sheltered him for so long.

"Tell us, Old Man," New Woman said as they walked. "What do you think the sun priest's vision really meant?"

He smiled somewhat sadly and shook his head. "I have been wrong before, but I'll tell you what I think. To him, the vision of mice was a good omen. He saw his people growing and multiplying, developing their skills and building their cities forever.

"To me, the vision of mice was not a symbol of his people at all. It was trying to warn him of a great plague that will come someday. Mice will come in from the desert and eat all the corn in the storage kivas. I tried to advise him to have them bring snakes into the kivas, to protect their grain as the Hohokam and the Mongollon do, but he laughed at me."

"What was it you said to him just before we left," Coyote asked.

"I told him to be less arrogant with his southern neighbors. His people may need them someday." He sighed.

"We have a long way to go to help our own people, my children. Let's hope we get there on time." The large group kept up a steady pace along the wide desert road as they made their way south.

CHAPTER 17

Large groups of holiday travelers passed them, making their pilgrimage to Half-Sun City. No wonder the high priest wanted to own that necklace and to own it now. Even though he had to give up Old Man to get it, the high priest would be the most resplendent of all the worshipers.

All the people they passed on the road were dressed in their holiday finery. They sang or played music as they walked. In front of each procession, children held small wooden staffs lined with small, ball-shaped objects made of copper. New Woman recognized the metal as the same material that made Tonkawa's cooking bowl. The balls must have contained pebbles because they emitted happy, tinkling sounds as the children shook the staffs.

Kataknek saw her looking back at them while the two groups passed each other. "Those are bells," he said. "Pochetas bring them from the lands to the south across the Great Gulf."

"A gulf?" New Woman asked, alert. "What is that?"

"A large amount of water, bigger than a bay, but with land on three sides. The land around this gulf would take months to walk around, so boats are made to cross it. I sailed across it once, long ago, on a reed boat. The Toltecs make large squares of woven reeds. They put them up on posts inside the boats so the wind can help push. That way, the rowers don't have to work so hard. They call the squares sails."

"That's amazing!" She tried to picture it in her mind.

"It only works when the wind is blowing the way you want to go. But it's a good idea when it works."

"Did they ever think of using cotton for the sails?"

"Hmm." Kataknek rubbed his chin. "I'll mention it next time a pocheta band passes through going south."

There is never an end to learning, New Woman thought. If only there were time to learn everything. Bells and gulfs and boats pushed by the wind. What wonders there were in the world!

Coyote caught up with them. He had been signing with some of the northerners.

"Tomorrow is Solstice Day. Old Man saw signs on the rocks when the sun rose this morning."

"Because of us, all these good people will have to spend the holiday on the road." New Woman sighed.

"No, we won't." Old Man had joined them. "There

155

will be people at the next city; the very old, the lame, anyone unable to make the journey and climb the steps over the cliffs. We'll help them celebrate."

They spent that night in one of the northern cities. The stay-at-homes were happy to share their special holiday treats when they saw the meat Coyote and some of the Hohokam priests and northern soldiers brought in from the desert.

They set about skinning the rabbits and the antelope for the solstice feast. New Woman was looking forward to reclaiming her bow. Anasi was taking care of it for her.

Long before dawn, Old Man and the priests rose and gave the word. Everyone who was able climbed up to the highest roofs to watch the sunrise. The gray sky lightened to a deep turquoise. The morning star faded. Rosy clouds heralded the dawn. Finally, the golden orb of the sun could be seen rising over the eastern hills.

"Praise to the sun," Old Man said in Hokan. "We thank you for another year of warmth and light. Continue in your goodness to us, honored one." He had no abalone shell here or holy sage leaves to burn. Coyote and New Woman joined him in a song of praise. The northern farmers and soldiers, and the Hohokam priests with Kataknek, said their own prayers, those that were familiar to them. The sun priests sang. Their voices blended into pleasing harmonies to honor the god they revered the most. In three languages, service to the sun was made.

They all ate together, the city dwellers of the north and the travelers. Everyone, New Woman noticed, gave praise to the brightest heavenly body on his longest day.

During the hottest part of the afternoon, most people retired for a midday nap. Coyote sat in the shade, resting

156

against a wall of one of the stone houses. He shut his eyes for a while. Then he took his flute from around his neck, where he wore it on a leather thong, and put it to his lips.

It was a thoughtful, questioning melody.

New Woman rested in the shade nearby. "What is it?" she asked when he put down his instrument.

"I can't get used to your new name. It's like you're someone else ever since you came out of the sun's house. We were friends. I don't know if we are anymore."

She did not know what to say. Her mouth hung open for a brief moment before she thought to close it. How could Coyote think they weren't friends?

"No. That's not true," she answered at last.

Coyote only shook his head. Then he lay back, his hands behind his head, to sleep out the heat of the day.

New Woman could not sleep, not now. She began to wander through the city. She had never really gotten to explore Half-Sun City. This one was much smaller. With most of its residents gone, it was no problem to walk through a number of the apartments.

The fire pits she saw were almost always on the first floors. The second-story rooms held the sleeping mats. She saw baskets and clay jars. Winter robes and summer clothing were stacked neatly on shelves. Weapons were hung from pegs on the walls. Doorways were high enough to allow a full-grown person to pass through without ducking. All the lower-floor rooms were connected by them.

Some of the rooms were stacked with corn. They contained grinding stones and bins. At home, the housewives gather together to grind acorn meal and gossip, New Woman thought. It must be very similar here when the women are home. She saw baskets filled with dried beans. Onions and peppers hung in nets on the walls to dry. Soon, there would be early squash. It was ripening even now in the fields.

She kept walking and thinking. The kivas must be empty now, with the worshipers gone. There would be no one to object if she entered one. She walked along them until she noticed one with part of its roof collapsed. This one certainly would not be in use even when the residents were home. It would have no holy objects inside she might profane.

She climbed down. With some surprise, she noticed a light. She saw an oddly shaped stone bowl. Part of a braided corn husk extended from an opening at one end. It was burning in what looked like water. This was impossible. Water put out fire. What magic made it keep burning?

She stood before it, studying the magic water. She was about to put a finger into the bowl when she was grabbed from behind and pulled back. Someone shouted something.

She found herself facing two girls and two boys of about her own age or younger. One of the boys spoke to her in the northern tongue. She did not understand a word he said.

"Do any of you know hand talking?" she signed. "I don't know your language. I'm a visitor here."

The tallest of the two girls touched her on the shoulder. "We all do. My friends"—she pointed to the others—"learned because of me. I am deaf."

New Woman looked well at them. The midday sun shining through the ladder hole and the place where the roof was broken added more light to the room. It was

158

enough to see that the boy who spoke first had a large purple birthmark that covered almost all of one cheek.

"Why are you here?" she gestured. "Why aren't you at the celebration in Half-Sun City?"

"You really are a foreigner," the deaf girl signed. "Don't you know that they don't like people who are different here? They don't want us at their celebrations."

New Woman never heard of such a thing. "What is different about you?" she asked the other girl. The girl walked into the shaft of sunlight and invited New Woman to come close. She pointed at her eyes.

"They're blue. Like the sky!" New Woman cried out loud in Hokan. She was shocked. No one had eyes that were anything but black or brown.

The girl did not understand the Hokan words, but she knew that tone of voice. "You hate me too," she signed. "Everyone hates me except for my friends here, but that's because they are all different too."

"I don't hate you. I was surprised," New Woman hurried to say. She held her hand out to the blue-eyed girl who had retreated to the wall. She smiled to her. "I don't hate you."

The girl shook her head, not believing. New Woman stepped up to her and took her hands, continuing to smile. Slowly, the girl smiled too. New Woman had to let go to sign again. "Your people are fools to hate you for this."

The last boy still stood by the wall, watching her suspiciously with large, frightened eyes. He looked about ten years of age.

"What is different about you?" she signed. He did not answer. Instead, he clenched his fingers and cowered, as if afraid of being struck. "Doesn't he know sign?"

The deaf girl tried to pull him forward. He attempted to shrug off her hands, but she persisted. At last, he allowed himself to be coaxed out of the shadows. He said a word in the northern language, a sharp, angry-sounding word. Then he held his two hands upright before his chest so she could see them. He had no thumbs.

New Woman made herself stand still. The people of this city must think these children had been cursed. No wonder they made them stay underground on the sun's day.

A thought flicked through New Woman's consciousness. If she had been influenced by anyone less than Momoy, she might have felt as the northerners did. She did not know how her own people felt about such things. Momoy herself was asked to leave her village. The old woman had taught her well. Different was all right. Sometimes, it was better. She wondered what Coyote would say now. Didn't he just tell her he wondered if they could still be friends, because she had changed, because she was different?

It was too complicated. She could not think. She only knew these young people had been wronged. "You are unhappy here." It was difficult to make a question out of it. It was a statement. She could only point to the boy and make the sign for brushing away a tear.

He bowed his head. Then he looked up again to see what she would do. She asked the same question of each of them, the boy with the birthmark, the girl with blue eyes, and the deaf girl. Each answered in the same way.

"I have only one friend right now, I think." New Woman pointed outside. "We are very far from home. If

160

my friend agrees, I will ask you to come back with me. Will the city let you go?"

"They would be happy. Why do you want us? Aren't you afraid?"

"I'm not afraid of you. I need people who know Corn Woman, people who can help me grow food. In my country, right now there is very little water and no rain. Can you help me?"

The deaf girl walked up to her. "Without enough food for your people, how will you feed us?"

"It can be done if we all help. You know how to grow food, don't you?"

"We grow our own," the deaf girl answered. "We are not permitted to eat from the city's fields."

"My people never had reason to grow food. It always came up by itself. The Chumash do not know planting."

At this, the four retreated to talk it over. The deaf girl returned in a few moments.

"We will consider what you offer."

New Woman understood. They wanted to be left alone to make a decision. Before she could leave, though, she had to try to understand the fire on the water. She walked back to it.

"Please, tell me how the water can let the fire burn. I never saw such magic," she signed.

The blue-eyed girl's eyes crinkled with merriment and the birthmarked boy began to chuckle. The blue-eyed girl signed to her, "It's not water." She took a small covered clay bottle from a recess in the wall. She opened New Woman's hand and poured a few drops of what looked like water into her palm. It was slippery between her fingers, like melted fat.

"We make it from corn," she said. "It's called oil, and this is called a lamp. It holds the oil so the piece of corn husk will keep burning until the oil is gone." She signed out the sentences, but used the northern language for the words *oil* and *lamp*. "There is little fuel here. We use this for light and save the rest for cooking."

New Woman had noticed few trees growing in this high, rocky country. For fuel, she saw people using corn husks. She admired the efficient use they made of all the parts of the corn. She admired many things she saw here.

"Thank you for telling me," she signed. It still seemed like magic, but she understood now that it was only a knowledge she did not share. With enough knowledge, anything might be possible.

"I'll ask you again before I leave if you want to come home with me," she said. Then she mounted the ladder.

The sun was a little lower when she found Coyote walking alone through the young rows of standing corn. She fell into step beside him. They walked together for a while, breathing in the smell of earth, of young growing things, and of desert air. They listened to the sound of insects. It was a bit like Momoy's garden, but different.

The corn itself was not the same. It was smaller, more compact. There were two corn plants and one bean vine growing between and around them on each small hill in the row. Each hill had in its center a depression covered with tiny stones from which the corn and beans grew. The earth must hold in the water better this way, New Woman guessed. The smaller corn made her think the seeds might be different than the ones the pochetas shared with Momoy, to be able to grow with less water.

"I'm having trouble getting used to my new name myself, you know," she mentioned casually, as if their earlier conversation had never been interrupted by Coyote's nap. He was in the act of stooping to sniff a squash blossom.

He rose. A stoic look of pain came over his face.

"But, I couldn't stay Child forever, could I?"

"It's not only your name, you know. It's everything. When we started out, you depended on me to guide you and protect you. Then Tonkawa made you his second-in-command."

"He did?" She was shocked.

"Of course he did. He asked you to tell him when his men were getting tired. You told the traders you would only take a man of your own people for a husband when you choose a man just to keep them from fighting over you. Then they all wanted you for their sister."

New Woman could barely keep up with his flow of words. It was as if someone opened the sluice in a Hohokam irrigation canal. How could he possibly think this? Before she could think how to answer him, he went on.

"I hardly believe you're Chumash anymore. You let Kataknek's wife turn you into one of them. The holy man and the priests all fawn on you. You traded with the high sun priest of the northerners like you were his equal. How can you possibly think I'm important enough to be your friend if you can do all this?"

"Are you finished?" she asked when he paused to take a breath.

"Old Man acts as if you were his wot."

She waited to see if there was going to be any more. Then she said softly, "He says I am to be one. It's written in the stars. But I'm nothing if I've lost my best friend." She might have been talking to herself. She didn't know if he even heard her.

He started to walk away again, slowly, with his head lowered. Was he angry or was he hurt? She walked after him. "Coyote," she said. He stopped, but he did not turn toward her. "Coyote, do you know how they treat people who are different here?"

The complete change of subject seemed to catch him off guard. "Different? How do you mean?"

"There are four young people, still children or barely into being adults, like me. I found them hiding in a ruined kiva today. They are not allowed to come out because it's Solstice Day. Their own people shun them: a boy with a big birthmark on one cheek, one with no thumbs, a deaf girl, and one with blue eyes."

"*Blue eyes!* No one has blue eyes."

"That's what I thought, until I saw her. How do we treat people who are different at home? I don't remember seeing any in the villages and then I lived with Momoy."

Coyote was still for a moment, his eyes closed. Then, "I've been throughout our lands and to the countries of our neighbors in the Big Valley and over the Southern Mountains on the plain. I saw people who were different. Some had scars or birthmarks. Some had something wrong with a leg or with an arm. Some were deaf and some were blind. The sun shines and the rain falls equally on everyone. I don't think the gods can be angry with them. A person does what he or she can to be useful and is helped by others when it's needed. The lazy are shunned in our lands, not people who are different."

It was a long speech for Coyote. Telling a story or bragging or complaining, those were a part of what made him unique. She knew he was not used to giving serious thought to differences among people.

164

She liked the way he expressed it. "The sun shines and the rain falls on everyone," she repeated. "That's the way you see it. That's the way I see it and that's how Old Man would see it. They don't look at it that way here. That's why I would never want to be anything but what I am and I would never want to live anywhere but in my own mountains by the sea.

"And," she added when she saw that she was getting through to him, "I would never accept for a husband a man who was not one of my own people. Remember what Kataknek said when his daughter decided to marry Okala? He said she couldn't do any better than to marry a pocheta. He said they would see each other enough to be happy, but never enough to grow tired of each other."

Coyote's eyes grew narrow. "You want to marry a pocheta? We have no long-distance traders among our people."

"I think you are the closest thing to it."

"What?!" She could almost see thoughts swimming in his eyes, like fish trying to catch up with each other.

"There's time to discuss that. I'm still very young and we have so much to get done, but I need you, Coyote. If I'm to be a wot, as Old Man told me he sees for the future, I'm going to need a lot of advice and friends. You're my very best friend. I need your advice right now about these four people. Don't ever desert me, Coyote."

"I thought you were deserting me," he said. Then he smiled. His white teeth lit up all of his bronze-colored, sun-darkened face. "Let's go meet these new friends of yours."

CHAPTER 18

More people were up and strolling
about to see New Woman and Coyote approaching the kiva. A skinny,
gray-haired old woman pointed
with a bony finger toward the place
and let fly with an emphatic group
of sentences.

"We don't know your lan-
guage," Coyote signed to her.

"Don't go there, foreigner," she
said in hand-talk.

Coyote shrugged and smiled.
New Woman made the "It will be
all right" sign before she mounted
the ladder. The woman shook her
hand at them and made growling
sounds.

"No animals here," Coyote
signed before he followed New
Woman. Just before his head dis-

appeared from her view, he grinned to her and waved.

New Woman found the children sitting on mats and tossing dice. They looked up as she approached, then looked curiously at Coyote. "I am called New Woman," she signed, saying the name in Hokan. "I forgot to tell you before. This is my friend, Coyote." She said the word, but made the sign for the animal. "He wants to be friends too."

The deaf girl rose from her mat and walked toward them, stopping in front of Coyote. "You are not afraid?"

"I'm hardly afraid of anything," he said, striking a brave pose. "I can fight ten Marauders with one hand tied behind my back." The girl laughed.

He tapped the deaf girl on the chest, saying "Hand-talk" in Hokan. He made the sign for the word. Then he pointed to himself, saying "Coyote," first the word, then the sign.

New Woman realized what he was doing. He was giving them Chumash names. He must agree with her, then! When he was done with Hand-Talk, he approached the boy with the purple mark on his cheek. "Cheek," Coyote said in sign and Hokan. He repeated the process, naming the girl with the oddly colored eyes Sky-Eyes.

Finally, he walked to the boy who had no thumbs on his hands. The youngster stared up at him, wide-eyed, too curious to be frightened. Before Coyote could name him though, the boy signed, "Are you the leader of your group?" He managed the signs awkwardly.

"No. New Woman is our leader." He signed "leader" but said "wot," so these Northerners would know his word for it.

"New Woman?" The four stared at her in disbelief.

"That's right," she signed. She could see it was a new idea to them, even here. The women may own the houses and the fields, but they must not usually govern the communities.

"Coyote," the thumbless boy continued, "are you a desert dog?" Coyote grinned. Then he put his hands to his mouth and gave the cry of the wild coyote people.

The boy laughed. He gulped in surprise at himself for laughing. Then he laughed again. At that, Coyote reached down, lifted the boy off his feet, and swung him in a circle, laughing too. The others joined in now, no longer shy of the foreigners. New Woman was glad. Only Coyote could have reached them this quickly and easily.

"You are Eight-Fingers," Coyote named him. "Now we are all friends. Do you want to go home with us? It's a long walk to the mountains near the big water. Many months of hard walking. Can you do it, little friend? Do you all want to come with us?"

"What will you do with us there?" Sky-Eyes asked. Coyote pointed to New Woman. She had to answer this.

"You'll help us plant corn, as I told you before, but only until the rains come again. After that, you will live the Chumash way. In my village, you will not have to hide away on special days. If anyone tries to hurt you, I will make *them* go. You can learn our language as we travel."

The four got into a huddle with their backs to Coyote and New Woman to talk again. When they were done, Sky-Eyes spoke for all of them.

"We will go."

"Come on, then. Let's climb up. You must meet our holy man." New Woman started to cross to the ladder.

168

"No," Cheek screamed. "They will throw stones at us if we come out today."

New Woman put her hand to her own cheek in horror. What kind of people were these Northerners to stone children?

"Wait then. I'll bring him to you." New Woman climbed out of the kiva to find it surrounded. Coyote was right behind her. "What do *they* want?" he whispered in her ear.

The woman who had warned them pointed and shouted triumphantly. She stood before the townspeople. The soldiers the high sun priest had lent them were milling about, not knowing what to do. The Hohokam sun priests were gathered close, trying to see if New Woman and Coyote needed help. Kataknek and Old Man stood nearby, in case translation was needed.

Kataknek pushed forward. "This old woman," he said, pointing to her, "says the witches have learned to change shape. They became animals. She says she heard them howling like desert dogs. We were all afraid they had killed you."

"No, Kataknek. That was us. We were only playing. There are only harmless children down there. They have certain differences, like being deaf or scarred. That seems to scare the people here. The children are so unhappy, Coyote and I decided to take them away to our country. They're coming home with us."

The three Northern farmers were standing close enough to see Kataknek's translation. If New Woman understood rightly, they were making a sign of protection against evil. The townspeople made the same sign. Some of them, at the first old woman's urging, were picking up stones.

169

"No!" New Woman screamed. She rushed at the woman and pulled away her stone. "They're only children. What's wrong with you?"

Old Man came up to stand beside her. He held his hands up to get everyone's attention. He was fluent in the Northern language. He signed as he spoke to make sure all understood. "We will leave now. If you are afraid of these children, you should be glad to see them go away."

The farmers, the soldiers, and the townspeople all began to speak at once. New Woman was glad to see the Hohokam priests remained quietly watching her. How annoying it was not to be able to speak and understand everyone. She waited for Old Man to give her an explanation.

"The farmers won't go any farther with us if you insist on bringing witches. The soldiers say the same."

"This has gone on long enough," New Woman said at last. "Kataknek, please bring me the captain of our guard from Half-Sun City. Then stay to translate."

The leader of the soldiers was brought before her. He was a slim, muscular man, probably in his thirties. He wore only a kilt and sandals, as did his men. He carried his half-length bow over one shoulder. A quiver rested on his hip. Hanging from his belt was a flint-tipped short spear.

"Please tell the captain that I am in charge of this expedition. The Hohokam priests can confirm what I say."

The man listened, but a smile began on his lips. New Woman tried to control her irritation.

"Your high sun priest," she continued, "swore to

me by the sun and the earth that we would have your protection until we reached the city of the Hohokam. I heard him say so to you before we left Half-Sun City. Will you make your high priest a liar?"

The man stood straighter when he understood her words. If he had thought he was there to humor the spoiled daughter of a wealthy nobleman, he appeared to be revising that impression. "He says he is honor-bound to keep his lord's word. He will protect you and do as you direct."

"Good," New Woman said. "Please tell him I say to control the townspeople and keep them out of our way. And tell him I say the children are coming with us."

The captain gave a few terse commands. One of the soldiers spoke sharply to the old people. When the first woman began to argue, half of the soldiers herded the townspeople into a far corner of the plaza in front of their houses.

They continued to make signs against evil. The first woman had them convinced. If they thought the children were cursed before, now they were positive that they were witches. New Woman had to take them now. The old people would either drive them out or stone them after she left.

"Coyote, please ask our new friends to come up now. I promise they will not be harmed. Tell them to bring what they'll need for the journey. We're leaving now."

The children emerged, hesitantly, ready to retreat or run if they needed to. New Woman went to greet them herself. Each one had a bundle wrapped in a sleeping robe. "Good," she signed. "Wait here."

"Captain, please bring the farmers to me now." By

171

the expressions on their faces, she could tell that the farmers' impression of her was also being revised. The three stood before her.

"Kataknek, please remind these good men that I paid for their services." When he had, she said, "Ask them if they are afraid of the children."

"These are not really children," came the translation. "They are witches. We will die if we take them with us."

When Kataknek finished, she said, "Tell me the truth, my friend. Do you believe what these farmers are saying?"

"I don't know," he confessed.

New Woman thought about that. Then she asked Kataknek to ask his high sun priest for permission to bring the children through the Hohokam city. She walked to the priest with Kataknek, according him respect by going to him rather than summoning him to her.

The priest spoke rapidly. Then he waited with his hands crossed on his walking staff. This was a holy man. He and Old Man were already becoming good friends. The priest kept his eyes on New Woman as Kataknek translated.

"Ever since you told me you dreamed of the Great Condor, not once, but twice, I knew you were not an ordinary young woman. Now, I have been privileged to see him with my own eyes. For my grandson, you jumped into the river. You pulled him away from the mouth of death. When I questioned you, I learned you would have done this for any child. You did not even know who he was. For your kindness and bravery the earth, the sun, and the sky must favor you. It is for this that we walked here with you and were not in our own city on Solstice Day. I believe you were sent here to save not only your holy man, but these children as well. Your friends will be welcome in my city."

She took the priest's hand in hers and smiled to him. "Thank you," she said in Hohokam. It was one of the few words of his language she had learned from Kataknek. "May Earth Mother give her blessings to your people forever." She had to sign the last. He nodded to show he understood.

New Woman continued to make the farmers wait. She walked next to the children. "Sky-Eyes, Cheek, Hand-Talk, Eight-Fingers," she addressed them. "These farmers are afraid of you. Can *you* direct us well enough to grow the corn?"

"We can," Hand-Talk motioned. When she looked at the farmers, her eyes were narrowed and her teeth were clenched. She sent a scathing look toward the frightened and angry townspeople as well before she looked back to New Woman. "We will do it for you and for Coyote. You're our friends."

"I put you in charge of our planting, then. You will direct my people and they will praise you for your knowledge."

She spoke at last to the farmers. "Bring me the three baskets of corn. Then you are dismissed." The farmers exchanged glances, confused. "Go." New Woman pointed back to Half-Sun City. The farmers ran for their packs as if afraid she was going to change her mind if they hesitated. They laid the baskets down before her, gave one more fearful glance at the children, and ran.

New Woman laughed. "Fools," she said aloud. "Kataknek, please tell your people and the soldiers that we are leaving. I won't spend another night in this city. Everyone must get his things. Let's see how far we can get today before we have to make camp."

Coyote, Old Man, and the children were lined up with their packs by the time New Woman returned to the plaza. The children held the baskets. "I brought a basket of beans," Eight-Fingers told her proudly while they waited for the rest. "It tastes good with corn." She squeezed his shoulder in approval. The boy beamed.

"If I doubted you had what it takes to be a wot," Coyote said to her, "I don't doubt it anymore."

New Woman was glad she had the soldiers with them when they walked through the wild country at the end of the Northern highway. She saw the Marauders counting their numbers and going away. Kataknek told her they were nomadic hunters of the great beasts called buffalo. "They fight each other over the herds, even though there are enough buffalo to cover all the land between here and the Great Water to the west. The herds move and their people must follow them. They never settle in one place. I think it keeps them mean and hungry. When they're bored with fighting each other, they attack travelers or try to steal from our cities. The Northerners have enough soldiers to protect themselves."

"Do you think they'll attack us when we go west? We didn't see any on our way to you. All the folk we passed were peaceful."

"They don't go where the buffalo can't graze. That's why the Northerners' roads and cities don't go east. Our cities don't go into the Great Prairies either. Those are Marauder lands. They have their own name for themselves, of course. Marauder is only the name we give to them. It means 'the wandering thieves.' "

She sent the soldiers home with her thanks when they reached the Hohokam city. The high priest took the children to his wife's house to bathe and rest until New Woman was ready to continue the next morning. There was no time to lose.

She was very happy to see Anasi and her children again. She let the woman bathe her and wash her hair once more, but when it was dry, she tied it back in her old way. The bangs had grown out and she tied the front in with the rest. "I want my mother to know me," she explained. She asked if she could use a cured skin she saw in Anasi's house. With it she made the two-piece apron that Chumash women wore. "This is how women dress in my country," she said. Her breasts were bare and free. "I want my friends to know me too."

She thanked Anasi and Kataknek for all they did. "I will never forget. I'll think of you with love whenever I remember my time with you."

Kataknek handed her a piece of hide with charcoal lines on it. "The sign for water is the sign for west. Follow this road to the Mojave. Ask one of them to draw you the best trail over the mountains. Always keep water with you. The desert in summer can be as dangerous as the mountains in winter."

Coyote smiled with pleasure as soon as he saw her. "That's my old friend," he said. "It's not the clothes that make you a woman anyway. It's what's under them."

"Now that's *my* old friend, Coyote. I would know you with my eyes closed." That made him smile even more broadly. Old Man and the children joined them, all of them carrying their packs.

New Woman looked back at the city, toward the

175

houses and the kivas, toward the fields bursting with food, and toward the dam that stored the water. It was good to have seen it, but it would be better to get home. "Good-bye," she said. They turned their faces toward the west.

CHAPTER 19

The journey home took longer than the journey out. The young Northerners had never traveled before. Eight-Fingers was only ten years old. Old Man had made this trip once when he was already getting on in his years. Now, he felt the aches and creaks of real old age in his bones.

They had to walk more slowly than New Woman would have wished, but she understood the necessity for it. They stayed several nights in the Mojave village the traders had passed on the way east.

The villagers remembered. They remembered how New Woman shared the last of her food with them and that she and Coyote showed them a good way to hunt rabbits. They fed the seven travel-

177

ers and gave them food to take with them. The Mojave children were well fed and sleek now.

The woman who once tried to bargain for New Woman's bow showed her a bow she had made for herself. "Some of my friends and I walked to the mountains for the wood," she explained in sign. "The foolish can use only spears if they wish. Now, I can feed my children better than before." She clasped New Woman's arm, happiness in her face. "Look at this." She gave a skin bag to New Woman and one to Coyote. "We found plenty. Eat these on your journey when you don't find meat." The bags were filled with pine nuts.

The Mojave young people found wonder and delight in the "magical" Northern children. They did not push them away. The curiosity they evoked made the others want to spend more time with them. Cheek and Eight-Fingers gloried in having friends. Sky-Eyes and Hand-Talk seemed hardly able to believe the shy smiles they were receiving from young Mojave men. New Woman was mildly surprised. The girls must have been older than they looked.

Before they left, Hand-Talk approached New Woman to ask her if she would accept two more young men into her band. "They wanted us to stay here. I told them we follow you to our new home. Now they want to come. They want to be our husbands."

New Woman was delighted for them, but she had to be sure they understood the situation. The two young men hung back. She approached them. "Will you accept my leadership? Will you agree to live in the ways of my people?"

The taller of the two signed, "I am called Road-Runner. We will live as our wives' people live. We will learn your language and help to find food. I accept you as my leader."

New Woman nodded her approval. She turned to the shorter of the young men. "I am Jumping Lizard," he said. "I accept your terms. I want Sky-Eyes for my wife. No other woman has eyes the color of turquoise stone. Everyone will envy me."

There were nine in New Woman's troop now. The young men made their farewells to their families. Half of the village came along to see them on their way to the mountains.

Bow-Woman gave New Woman a map drawn in charcoal of the way to the next village. "May Earth Mother and Sky Father guide you and yours," Bow-Woman said when she and the others were ready to turn back.

"May you and yours always have enough to eat," New Woman returned, holding her hands out over the earth.

Little by little, their footsteps brought them closer to home. They rested often and camped early when Old Man became tired. The desert and the mountains were finally crossed. The long plain was at last before them.

Seasons changed while they walked. The leaves colored and fell. Flocks of geese flew overhead when the winds became colder. Coyote, New Woman, and the others had success in the hunt more often than not. Eight-Fingers grew taller.

All of them, even Old Man, found their walking legs. The Northerners learned Hokan. Old Man proved an excellent teacher. His students made rapid progress. Hand-Talk had no trouble, since her talk was the same in any language. Road-Runner and Hand-Talk would never have been able to converse without it.

The geese were flying north again when New

Woman, Old Man, and Coyote stepped once again on the foothills of their homeland.

Old Man knelt and placed both hands flat to the ground. New Woman and Coyote followed him immediately. Cheek, Eight-Fingers, Hand-Talk, Sky-Eyes, and their husbands were not at all surprised to see tears in the eyes of the three as Old Man led them in a prayer of thanksgiving.

"We're almost home now," New Woman told her people. "I expect there will be less food than normal, so when we pass through villages, and we're invited to share food, I ask that you watch how much the villagers take. If they do with small portions, don't take more. They have little to spare."

Instead of the profusion of wild grasses and flowers of early spring after a winter of rain, the hills were the spare and dreary brown of late summer.

"Listen," Coyote said. There were fewer insects in the grass and flying through the air. The travelers saw few birds and heard less chirping from within the chaparral.

"Look," Coyote said. A family of coyotes walked on the crest of the next hill. They were thin and had only one pup.

"The mother didn't have enough milk for her children, Coyote," Old Man said. The stream beds were almost dry. "Look at these leaves." He broke a few from a nearby ceanothus bush. They crumbled into dust in his hands.

"Look at these acorns." New Woman bent, picked some off the ground, and turned them over. "They're full of dust. There aren't even any worms inside. Why is this happening, Old Man?" Her voice rose as she asked.

"Sky Father is angry. He's keeping the clouds away." Old Man raised his eyes to the harsh blue of the empty sky. "Old Man Sun is punishing the land. He comes too close with his firebrand, and Earth Mother doesn't seem to care."

"She could make them behave if she wanted to." Coyote picked up a stone and threw it angrily as far as he could.

"She must be angry also," New Woman said sadly.

Hand-Talk came up to Old Man. "You knew. You were so far away in Half-Sun City, but you knew. You are truly a holy man. Maybe she is angry because you were sent away." She stroked his cheek reverently. She knew he continued to tell his stories in the sign language, even after the others learned Hokan, just so she would never feel left out.

He pushed her hair back from her face. It was flying like a dark cloud around her in the dry wind.

"Let's go to Momoy's valley. I hope it's not too late for us to help." He put his walking staff before him. "From here, I can find the way."

New Woman touched the trees on both sides of the trail. It was like seeing old friends again. "Wait," she whispered to a dry birch. Only a few buds were trying to grow on some of its branches. "Don't die," she told it. "The rains will come again. You too," she told a walnut tree. "Have patience. Wait for the rain."

A woman was digging watercress near Momoy's spring. The little pond was still bubbling. "Thank the gods," Old Man said. "This one hasn't dried up."

"Oh," exclaimed the woman, turning around and seeing them. "I didn't know there were strangers in the valley."

"Will you please bring us to Momoy," New Woman asked politely.

"Certainly." The woman slung her small burden basket over a shoulder. Using her digging stick for a staff, she led them toward Momoy's house. The trees and bushes here were doing well. Even the cornstalks were high and green.

Sky-Eyes reached for New Woman's arm. "There is corn here." The question hung between them.

"This is Momoy's garden. Only she may work it. She is Corn Woman's sister. None of my people may grow corn. It is forbidden because Corn Woman herself never gave us permission. That is why I needed people from Corn Woman's own land to plant enough corn for all of us. We can help you with the irrigation and the cultivation if you'll show us how. Once the rains come, and the oak trees give us good acorns again, our corn must be eaten entirely and never be planted again."

"I understand you now," Sky-Eyes said. The others listened and nodded as it became clear.

The woman led them to an aisle in the garden. "Momoy, there are people here to see you." Then she stepped aside.

The two women saw each other. "Mother!" screamed New Woman.

"Oh Child. My child!" They fell upon each other, laughing, touching, and crying. "Child, we wondered if we'd ever see you and Coyote again."

"My name isn't Child anymore, Mother. It's New Woman now. I found the man whose spirit called to mine. He's right here. Mother, this is Old Man."

The older woman looked at Old Man as if she saw

a ghost. She seemed to freeze. Her eyes opened their widest.

Old Man walked up to her and took her trembling hands. "It's really me, Pretty One," he said gently. "I've come back. Your daughter was the child I saw in my vision almost fifteen years ago. She's the child of the prophecy. You heard of the prophecy?"

"Oh, yes." She spoke at last. "But how can it be?"

"Everything I saw was true. Even though the prophecy is not yet complete, every fact was accurate, but one. I saw your daughter in my vision dressed in man's clothes in a foreign land. I saw her wearing her hair in the manner of the long-distance traders. I thought I saw a boy. Because I told Swordfish what I saw, everything else followed."

He hung his head before her. "I beg you to forgive me for what you suffered."

"Look at me, Old Man." He raised his eyes to her face. "You brought my daughter home. I would forgive you anything." She turned to her daughter again, looking to see the difference one and a half years had made.

"You've grown," she said. "I was afraid that meeting new people and seeing the cities would change you. I'm glad to see that you are still one of us." She extended one arm toward her daughter. New Woman walked into it.

"Mother?" she asked. "Why did the woman who brought us to you call you Momoy? Where is my grandmother?" There was a question, unspoken, in her eyes, the one she was afraid to ask out loud.

Mother laughed. "Oh, no. Let me explain. It's not what you think. Momoy is called Old Momoy now, and

I'm called Young Momoy. You aren't the only one who can change her name, my daughter. Mother Momoy is around here somewhere."

She called to someone. "Please bring my mother to me." New Woman let out her breath in a huge rush. She hardly realized she was holding it.

Old Momoy stepped into view a few moments later. "Well, you lazy old Coyote," she said, grabbing the surprised Coyote in a crushing hug. "I thought you'd never get around to bringing my granddaughter back to us."

Coyote swallowed, trying to take a breath. The hug had knocked the air right out of him. "It's nice to see you again too, you snake-haired, frog-voiced, scrawny-necked old woman."

"Granddaughter," she said, letting go of Coyote at last. She put her cheek to New Woman's and hugged her only a little less violently than she had Coyote. "I see you brought guests home with you."

She turned to look at them. Then she swallowed and froze, just as Young Momoy had done. She blinked. He was still there. "Old Man?" she asked hesitantly. New Woman had never heard her grandmother's voice go gentle like that.

"Are you really here or is an old woman's eyes playing tricks on her?"

"I'm really here, my old friend." He took her into his arms. New Woman saw and turned away her eyes. These two had once been more than friends.

After all the new people were introduced, New Woman told her mother and her grandmother what she intended to try to do with the newcomers' help. Old Momoy nodded. "It might work." She called a few people to her side and gave orders. "Start food cooking. Everyone eat. Coyote, walk up to Crab's village. Tell him I call a meeting after supper. We must make plans."

It was good to eat familiar food again. New Woman smacked her lips over the acorn gruel. "It tastes like home. Enjoy it, there's plenty," she said when she saw the Mojave men and her northern friends eating less enthusiastically. She signed the same words to Hand-Talk to make sure she understood.

"We'll have to get used to your food as you did to ours," Hand-Talk signed back.

"You will." New Woman scraped out the last little bit from the bottom of her bowl.

Sunflower ran up to her as soon as she was finished. Her two boys were walking already. They followed with Crab.

"Oh, I'm so glad to see you again," Sunflower said as she moved back from New Woman's welcoming embrace. "Coyote said your name is New Woman now. You really are. I still remember when I carried you for your mother. Now you're old enough to have your own baby."

New Woman laughed. "Fourteen is still young. I have time for that. Just look how your boys are growing up."

Sunflower patted her tummy proudly. "Crab and I hope our next one is a girl. Coyote said Old Man is here too. Everyone thought he died when he went away. Oh." She giggled. "I guess you're too young to remember that."

She saw him and went over to welcome him, smiling a shy greeting. He surprised her with a gentle hug.

Two Leaves, Sunflower's mother, was here also, as was Sunflower's father. Crab's mother and father, one of his sisters, and the sister's husband were here. A real village had grown where the two outcasts had camped.

185

They had a siliyak, and a dancing floor; even a small cemetery had been started when one of the hunters of Crab's village was found mauled by a bear.

Sunflower filled them in on the gossip. Crab came to welcome New Woman home too. He had always been kind to her. In a way, he had taken the place of an older brother to her since she was five. "I see you still carry your bow," he said. "You haven't forgotten how to hunt."

"Your teaching kept hunger away on the trail, Crab. You were always my friend." It was, indeed, a happy homecoming.

Old Momoy called Crab and the Antap of his village to sit before her house. "My granddaughter, New Woman, has something to tell you."

New Woman explained her idea. "If you agree to help, we can prevent many deaths this year from the famine. We think the earth is angered by the feuding between your village and Seahawk's and between Seahawk's and Swordfish's. If peace comes, she may relent and let the rains come back. In the meantime, these friends I made in the eastern countries may be able to help."

She introduced them. "These people have been given permission from Corn Woman, a daughter of Earth Mother, to grow corn. The seeds they brought with them from their country need even less water than Momoy's corn. I want them to tell us how to prepare the ground, but *they* must plant it.

"With Earth Mother's permission, it will grow. We must share with all who are hungry, even those from Sa'aqtik'oy and Wene'mu, as soon as they are willing to put an end to war. We hope this will please the earth enough so that she will allow rain to come, so we can

186

go back to our own ways. "Will you and your people help, Crab?"

"We must talk, New Woman," he said. She could only hope he would see the merit in her plan. He had reason to hate Seahawk, who had driven his family away.

He called the Antap of his village to him. Then he gathered the rest of them, apparently asking their opinion.

"He is a good wot," she remarked to Momoy and her mother while they waited. "He asks the priests for their advice."

Crab returned, looking meaningfully at New Woman. "For the sake of peace, would *you* be able to forgive Seahawk? Would you be able to forgive Swordfish? Would you, Young Momoy?"

Young Momoy walked to Crab, her mouth set in a determined line. New Woman had heard her mother speak her mind before. She waited.

"Crab," Young Momoy stated regally, her head held proudly, "for the sake of peace, I hid my disgrace from my own brother for five years. If it will keep children from going hungry, I will forgive. Even Swordfish."

Crab, ashamed, lowered his head for a moment. Then he looked into her face. "It was never your disgrace. It was always his. *You* should have been made wot of Sa'aqtik'oy. If you can forgive, so can I. New Woman, the Antap agreed to allow me to accept you as our pacwot. I will continue to be wot of my village, but you are my leader. We will do as you suggest."

New Woman came forward and put her hands in his. "Good. Tomorrow, the planting will begin."

187

CHAPTER 20

Cheek was the oldest Northerner. Jumping Lizard and Road-Runner were older, but New Woman had directed that the Northerners, not the Mojaves, were the planting leaders. In Cheek's country, as in the Hohokam and the Mongollon cities, it was the men who put the seeds into the ground.

Cheek directed his workers in the preparing of the ground. The earth mark on his cheek gave the people confidence. When the land was broken and cleared, the people made rows of small hills. They poured small amounts of water in each hill. The women sang to make the earth ready.

The seeding was done the next day. Cheek placed two corn seeds in each prepared hill. Eight-Fingers followed, placing a bean next to the corn. The planting was done in one day, first in the small field of Momoy's valley, then in the larger one, where the playing field had been beside Crab's village.

Sky-Eyes and Hand-Talk led a line of children through the newly planted furrows. Mothers carrying babies and most especially pregnant women followed them. Sky-Eyes and Hand-Talk allowed their long hair to brush the ground. Sky-Eyes sang in the Northern tongue. Hand-Talk put the words into sign.

New Woman watched from the side with Coyote, her mother and grandmother, and Old Man. Around her were many who did not know the sign language, so she translated. "She's saying, 'Corn Woman, thank you for your gift to us. Earth Mother, give us your blessing and make this corn grow.'"

Sky-Eyes sang the words a few times and then hummed, so everyone could join her in the song.

"You say these people were outcasts in their own city?" Momoy asked. She tapped her stick to the rhythm of the song.

"That's right."

"I hope the fools get what they deserve someday."

When the first shoots came up, the Northerners danced through the rows again. They taught the Chumash how to tell corn and bean shoots from weeds. Part of the dance was the weeding. "Sky Father, bring rain clouds," they sang.

Cheek and Eight-Fingers showed how to make a ditch from the pool under the waterfall and from the spring, to bring the water where it was needed. It was hard work to dig the channels. The strong and healthy felt the sweat pouring when they straightened up after the back-straining labor.

Momoy's corn was harvested and the new corn put into her garden too. Only a small portion was reserved for her special flowers.

"We will have two, maybe three plantings," Cheek explained to New Woman. "There will be more than enough to feed all your people. Enough to feed three times the people here and in Crab's village."

"Then there will be the right amount."

"I don't understand," Cheek said.

"When the time comes, if things go as I hope, you will."

Both Sky-Eyes and Hand-Talk found they were pregnant when the corn flowers opened. "This is very lucky," Cheek told New Woman. "It means the corn will be fruitful like the women. Maybe I will marry also. You have pretty women here in Chumash country."

"This is your home now too," New Woman reminded him. "I hope you will be happy here."

"You and Coyote led us out of darkness. I hope your people will be happy. I'm glad I can help."

New Woman was glad they had learned the language so well. All of the newcomers were made to feel welcome. Cheek still said "your people." She hoped the time would come when he would say "our people."

Even little Eight-Fingers made friends. He was no longer the frightened, angry boy of the ruined kiva. He ran and played as hard as any of the other boys in his age group. His lack of thumbs interested them for a while. Then, one of the other boys fell on a rock. It opened his cheek. Old Momoy had to make a strong concoction of her flower root to make him sleep while Two Leaves sewed the gash closed with yucca fiber. His stitches made him the newest sensation among the playmates. Soon Eight-Fingers' difference was ignored as he ran, climbed, and played with the rest of the children.

One evening, late into summer, he came up to her. "Is it all right if I go with my friends? They're going to the ocean tomorrow. I haven't seen it yet."

She was startled. "We're keeping you too busy then. Once the drought is over and food comes up by itself, you'll have more time for fun. No more planting and weeding and digging irrigation canals. Of course, go with them. Pack a picnic basket. While you're down there, dig some clams, will you? I haven't eaten any in so long."

"If there are any clams down there, I'll find them so I can bring you some," he promised. "What's a clam?"

She laughed. His accent was so good and he was fitting in so well, she had almost forgotten he wasn't born Chumash. "The others will show you."

When the corn flowers opened, the northerners did a thing even Old Momoy had never seen. They picked certain of the blossoms and touched them to the others. "It's a marriage of the flowers, so the corn will grow if there are not enough insects," Cheek explained when she asked.

Young Momoy stood with New Woman by the doorway to their keesh. "Your friends are happy here," she said. "It's time you knew Mother Momoy and I are going to leave after the rains come back and our land returns to normal."

"Mother!" New Woman was startled at this news.

"Mother Momoy likes privacy. There are too many people here now. We'll tell you when we find a new

191

valley, where we can raise our flowers in peace. We'll be sorry to give up this valley, but it's for a good cause."

New Woman saw that her mother had found fulfillment in the carrying on of Momoy's tradition. It was good.

Bins were made to hold the harvested corn where animals could not get at it. Hand-Talk and Sky-Eyes showed the Chumash women how to grind the dry kernels and how to make the flour into cereal and bread. The fresh corn they cooked with beans and onions.

The next time a clamming party set out, New Woman told the leaders of the group not to avoid other groups. "Tell them we have plenty of food here. Show them the way back if they ask. Draw a picture of the trail on the sand." She hoped to bring the villages of Sa'aqtik'oy and Wene'mu to peace with the offer of food.

A few more people came to them. New Woman learned from them that there had been several rainfalls in the north. The villages there were not in so dire a situation. Both Swordfish and Seahawk sent traders to buy food with shell money. They were trying to wait out the drought.

Coyote and New Woman went for a walk through the fields. "When I look around at this, I feel like I'm back in the cities," Coyote said. People were weeding and deepening the ditches. "It's too much work. When will we get back to normal? When will we have acorn mush to eat again?"

"But, Coyote," New Woman said mockingly. "You don't like acorn mush. You only like meat."

He looked around quickly. "Did anyone hear me say that? Acorn mush is good enough, I guess, to wash the meat down. There isn't enough meat either. The animals went north, where the grazing is better. The fishing is better there too. In Wene'mu, they're living on clams."

"You've been there?" She was so busy. She remembered now, she hadn't seen him in several days. "How are they getting along? How is my uncle Seahawk?"

"He's getting angry because more of his people are coming here. I told him Crab's village has enough food to share with them. He won't admit he was wrong to drive Crab away for disobeying him. Now his people are suffering for it. He's a stubborn old fool."

Before New Woman could respond, he said, "Swordfish knows there is a valley here with food. He doesn't know whose valley it is, but he doesn't want to admit he can't take care of his people. He's another stubborn fool."

For years, Coyote had known Swordfish was New Woman's father, ever since he brought up the topic in Momoy's keesh when New Woman was eleven.

"Why can't they see that they are the cause of the problem?" New Woman was almost ready to cry in exasperation. "Won't they ever make peace? Coyote, what will it take to bring them together?"

"I don't know." He pulled her closer to him. They stood together, side by side, comfortable just being together. "It will have to work out. We've gotten this far, haven't we?"

New Woman looked up to the path on the ridge above the valley. It felt good to rest her head against Coyote's shoulder. They had come far. She took a deep breath.

"What is that?" She was suddenly alert. "That's not a cooking fire. I smell smoke."

"Let's climb to the top of the ridge. Maybe we can see where it is." Coyote began as he spoke. They scrambled up the hill, sniffing. The higher they climbed, the more they could feel the hot, dry wind that was blowing. The steep hills that sheltered the valley cut it off from above, but if the wind should blow it toward them . . . New Woman was afraid to finish the thought.

There was a plume of smoke rising rapidly in the north and growing darker. Birds were flying before the smoke, coming toward the valley and going beyond, to the ocean.

"The mountains are tinder after so much dryness," Coyote said. "The fire will burn whichever way the wind blows. Nothing can stop it but the ocean."

"Oh, no. Coyote, we have to warn everyone. Can we get to Sa'aqtik'oy in time?"

"They know. The fire is near them. Look." Black puffs of smoke mixed with the white that was swiftly covering the northern sky. "That'll be the houses."

"Holy Mother," New Woman exclaimed. "Please, save them. Can we warn Wene'mu, do you think?"

"I don't know. I'll try, if you want."

"I'll bring our people down near the spring. That should be the safest place. Maybe we'll be lucky and the wind won't bring the fire this way."

They both had taken a few steps when the same thought occurred to them. Coyote and New Woman stopped to look back at each other. One of them might not make it. New Woman ran to him. There was no time for more words now. A quick embrace and Coyote was on his way, running lightly over the mountains to Wene'mu.

New Woman tried to think of the best course of action while she ran back to the lower valley. Old Momoy had a conch shell in her keesh. It was the fastest way she could think to summon everyone. She hoped the noise she could make with it would bring Crab and his people. It had never been used for this before.

Her mother was standing before the doorway, sniffing the air, a worried look on her face.

"Mother," New Woman said, "the mountains are on fire. I'm going to blow the conch."

"Where is Coyote?" Old Momoy asked as she ran up to them.

"I sent him to try to warn Wene'mu," New Woman said. The old woman bit her lip and looked toward the sky.

New Woman emerged, holding the large, convoluted shell. Before the last bellowing notes died away, the people of Momoy's valley were before her and folk were running down the path from Crab's village as well.

Crab ran up to her. On his back, and on the backs of the adults who weren't carrying children, were baskets filled with ears of dried corn. "We saw the smoke," he said. "Do you know where the fire started?"

"Coyote and I climbed up on the ridge. It's in the north, but it's moving fast. We think it passed through Sa'aqtik'oy." A few of the nearby people began to wail. Friends and family had been left behind when they came to Crab's village. Some of the children started to cry.

"Let's all stand as close to the spring as we can. If the fire comes here, we can at least try to save ourselves," New Woman said.

The smoke covered the sky to the northwest now.

They heard the crackling of the fire. Old Man instructed the children and the parents holding babies to stand closest to the water.

The air and the mountains seemed to come alive. After the birds, flies and wasps filled the air. Mosquitoes buzzed and landed on the water. Frightened deer and mountain goats scrambled down to the uncertain shelter of the valley. Rabbits were close behind them.

Mountain lions and wolves came running before the fire. The coyote family Coyote saw when they arrived in the early spring scampered into view. The lone cub was almost grown. A bear lumbered down the steep trail, pushing her young before her. Squirrels chittered as they practically flew through the brush away from the fire. Even snakes were slithering down the hills into the lower valley.

New Woman could see the tongues of the fire from where she stood. They were licking the chaparral up on the ridge, a bright orange against the black, ash-filled sky. Old Man, Old Momoy, New Woman's mother, Two Leaves, and Sunflower led the people in a prayer chant. Several Antap priests from Sa'aqtik'oy and Wene'mu were there as well. All of them lent their voices to a plea for protection. There was no fighting such a fire.

New Woman's friends from the eastern lands looked fearfully up to the hills. They had never seen a fire out of control. There was so little in their desert and stony homes to burn. Eight-Fingers sidled up and slipped his fingers into New Woman's hand. "Are we going to burn up?" he asked. Had she brought all of them here only to die?

"No!" she said emphatically. "If we have to, we'll get in the spring where the fire can't follow us." And breathe in the smoke until we die, she added in her thoughts.

"Pray to whichever god you think will hear you to make the wind blow it away. If the fire goes to the ocean, it will have to stop."

Eight-Fingers screwed up his eyes in concentration and moved his lips. Then, he smiled. "New Woman!" he shouted. The others looked toward him also.

"The fire won't come here. I know."

Old Man was standing close to them. "How do you know that, Eight-Fingers?"

"Because *she* told me."

The crackling sound grew fainter. New Woman closed her eyes and strained her ears to listen. The sounds had changed. She opened her eyes and looked up to where she had seen flames only moments before. They were gone.

"The fire went away," Eight-Fingers said. "I told you."

"Look!" New Woman pointed to the sky. The billows of brown-gray smoke were crowding toward the southwest. A patch of blue opened as they watched, breaking through the ash-filled haze. The sun's rays filled the valley.

New Woman raised her hand to her eyes to block out the glare. "It passed us!" someone shouted.

"The wind changed," Old Momoy said quietly. There was cheering and laughing all around them. The danger was over.

Old Man led them in a song of thanksgiving. Eight-Fingers touched her arm. "I asked Earth Mother, the one you call Chupu, because you love her best. She answered me. Do you think I might become a priest like Old Man is, someday?"

In his own country, he had been an outcast. Here, he could go wherever his spirit called. This, from the boy who had to hide his disfigurement on Solstice Day.

"Soon it will be time for your vision quest. When the time comes, Momoy will give you a special drink. When you find your spirit guide, you must ask. I think you will be a very strong holy man. The Mother does not often speak to boys who are only eleven years old."

He ran off with his friends. That was as it should be. The fire was not out yet. Would the marshes of Wene'mu kill it, or would the wind push it all the way to the ocean? One more thought worried New Woman. Was Coyote all right?

CHAPTER 21

New Woman, Crab, and many others climbed the trail to the ridge the next morning. Black grass continued to smolder in places. In the still air, clumps of chaparral burned themselves out. The earth looked dead.

New Woman's mother stood beside her. "This has happened before, Daughter, and it will happen again. When I was a girl, I saw where a fire had burned after a lightning storm. My first mother, the grandmother you never knew, told me the land would come alive again when the rains came. I thought nothing would ever grow there again, but I was wrong. We'll see flowers again, even here, when the rains come."

"*If* the rains come, Mother."

New Woman's voice grew tight. Even the animals who had taken shelter with them were gone now. It hurt to look at the desolation.

"It will rain again," Old Momoy said firmly. "We wouldn't have been spared from the flames if our mother, the earth, intended to let us starve in the end. If it never rained again, even my spring would dry up." Old Momoy smiled through her wrinkles. New Woman sometimes thought she could see a young woman looking out of her grandmother's eyes. "When the land has returned to normal, it will be time for your mother and me to look for another home."

New Woman had accepted it, but the idea of their leaving still made her sad. "I shall miss you," she said simply.

"Oh, you'll see us again. I'll expect visits and reports on how you're doing."

"And I'll want to see my grandchildren some day," her mother added. "We'll let you know how to find our new valley."

New Woman looked around her at the charred earth, and sighed. Coyote is out there somewhere, she thought. Would there ever be grandchildren to show her mother?

Young Momoy was looking the other way, toward the ocean. On a far-distant ribbon of trail, she saw a band of people walking through the smoke and the haze toward them.

"Look, Daughter." She took New Woman's arm and turned her to see. "Look who's coming to us." There were hundreds of them, young and old, stooped with walking sticks and straight with burden basket or child on their hips or backs. "By the spirits, all of Wene'mu is coming here and my brother is leading them."

200

New Woman strained her eyes. "And Coyote is leading him!" she shouted happily. Old Momoy took her young hand and squeezed it. They both murmured silent thanks.

"Crab!" New Woman called. He came up beside them to watch also. His face was immobile, but New Woman could imagine the thoughts that must be there. It was not easy for him either.

Seahawk stopped his group short of the ridge that led down to the valley. He walked forward alone. Coyote stood back with the villagers, but he threw a smile to Old Momoy and a wink to New Woman.

Before Seahawk could speak, he recognized his sister and his niece standing beside Crab. Young Momoy whispered something to Crab and then walked directly to him.

"You are unhurt, Brother? Your people? Did any die in the fire?"

"I am unhurt," he said. "My people all live."

"What did the fire do to Wene'mu?"

Seahawk cleared his throat. "Wene'mu is gone, Sister. We stood in the ocean by the tomols and watched it burn to the ground."

Young Momoy gave a long sigh. "It was once my home too. Come, Brother. You must speak to Crab now."

The two men looked at each other. Crab stood still. Seahawk walked up to him and spoke first. "I wronged you."

New Woman watched her uncle's jaw trembling. How hard this must be for him.

Before Crab could answer, Seahawk swallowed and spoke again. "I am stepping down. My son, Otter, is the new wot of the people of Wene'mu. He will ask you to

201

feed and protect our people. If you wish, I will leave, but don't turn my people away. Coyote said there is food to spare in this valley. Please, don't hold the anger you have for me against the others."

Seahawk, having spoken, would have stepped back to make room for his son, but Crab took his arm, gently but firmly.

"Stay," he said. "This is Momoy's valley, not mine. She let us make use of it because we were homeless. Anyone who enters Momoy's valley is welcome to shelter and food and forgiveness, if he will accept the peace of this place and of New Woman. She is responsible for our having food here. I am wot of my people. She is pacwot."

"New Woman?" Coyote had not told him.

"Hello, Uncle," she said, walking up to give him a quick embrace. "I'm New Woman."

"By all the stars! Is this the child who rode to Wene'mu like a big fish in my burden basket?"

New Woman laughed. "The very same. Otter! Cousin!" she called. "Come. I want to see you. My uncle tells me you're wot now."

The young man came up to her. Seahawk stood back.

"Cousin?" he asked. "You're Child? What happened to you?" He saw a tall, self-assured young woman, no longer in any way a girl.

"I grew up. I'm called New Woman now. We have enough food and shelter for all. I am pacwot to Crab's village. Will you accept me as your pacwot too, and will you accept the peace of Momoy's valley for all your people?"

"What do you mean?"

202

"No more war. Everyone helps each other. All wots accountable to me."

It was a new idea after so long. Otter smiled and held out his hand. New Woman took it. "I accept," he said. He turned back to his people. "We're all friends again. We are welcome."

Coyote came up to New Woman to help her and Crab lead the new people down to the valley. She leaned her forehead against his shoulder for a brief moment. "I'm glad to see you again," she whispered. He touched her back.

She looked over the refugees before they began the descent. Her aunts looked less proud now. Both of them lowered their eyes before her mother. That was good. Her old friends were here too. She could tell they were trying to see their old friend in the imposing woman she seemed to them now. There was time to renew the old friendships.

She looked back over the line, trying to pick out familiar faces. Crow Eyes, the storyteller who had warned her about Momoy so many years ago, tottered along, helped by her children and her grandchildren. Many of them appeared to be in shock.

In the valley, they were given the crisp, flat corn bread with onions and beans to eat. Many of them shook their heads with disbelief at the strange sight of planted rows of food.

New Woman brought Otter to meet Cheek and the others after he had eaten and quenched his thirst. "Uncle, you come too." He had been sitting with her mother.

"I've heard about your travels," he said while they walked. "You brought this special knowledge back to save our people."

203

"Otter. Uncle"—she stood still—"this is special knowledge, but it's not mine. It's not Chumash. When the rains come again and the acorns are full once more, we must not plant corn again. The special seeds that made these plants are from Cheek's people." They stood before the young man now.

"Cheek, please come meet my uncle and my cousin, the wot of these people." "Hand-Talk," she signed, "come too. Bring Road-Runner. Sky-Eyes, please bring Jumping Lizard and come to meet Seahawk, my uncle, and Otter, wot of Wene'mu." Eight-Fingers was near. "Come," she said, motioning for him to come over.

She introduced them all. "These are the Mojaves and the Northerners. It is their knowledge that made this food. They made the planting. Corn Woman revealed the secret of planting to their people. They came to do this for us."

Otter went to each of them in turn to give thanks. He took a step back when he saw Sky-Eyes' bright blue eyes. He swallowed when he saw Eight-Fingers' hands. He saw the earth mark on the side of Cheek's face.

"You are the chief planter. I thank you." Then he moved to Hand-Talk. "Thank you," he said.

"You must use sign," Road-Runner said. "She can't hear anything."

"I'll have to learn it," Otter said. "Please tell her thank you for me. Are all people from the east magic?"

New Woman saw him struggling with his feelings. The biggest of these seemed to be awe. He was raised on Crow Eyes' stories. He hardly seemed able to believe he was standing in Momoy's own valley.

Cheek came up to him again. "We're not magic. We are only different. We come from a far land. Your spirit of the earth saved us from the fire yesterday. She allowed our corn to grow here. Now, I know it will rain again. We won't plant anymore. We are Chumash too, now."

Hearing these words meant more to New Woman than anything else he might have said. She smiled, and took his hands in hers. "We are all one people," she said. "We work, and live, and are happy together. All will be well."

The day was spent renewing old acquaintances. The people of Crab's village showed the people of Wene'mu how to clear the silt and ash from the irrigation ditches and how to weed. The women were shown how to grind the unfamiliar corn. Soon, we will have acorns again, New Woman thought. If only Swordfish would give in and bring his people also.

Some of Crab's villagers were less happy. She could see their worry. She called over a few of the young people who had left Sa'aqtik'oy to join the village in Momoy's valley recently. "Do you know who I am?" she asked when they were together.

"You are New Woman," one of them answered. "Crab told us you are pacwot, leader to Crab and now to Otter, the wot from Wene'mu. What do you want us to do?"

"Before I tell you that, I must tell you something else. I was born in Sa'aqtik'oy, like you. It was my first home. When I was five, I went to live in Otter's village by the sea. The home of my youth means very much to me," she said. They were looking at her with greater interest now. She saw their faces working, trying to remember her.

"There is no reason for them to go hungry," she continued. "I want you all to go there and try to find them. We believe the village was destroyed by the fire.

Please, tell Swordfish he is welcome to come here. We have enough food for everyone. We'll find homes for them until they can rebuild on their own mountain. Tell Swordfish that his daughter invites him to share bread."

One of the young women stared at her now with big, round eyes. She put her hand to her mouth. "You're my friend, Four Cries, who went away!" She began to sway on her feet. New Woman rushed up to steady her. The young woman began to cry. "I'm the one who told you about Swordfish and your mother when we were digging onions."

New Woman put an arm around her old friend. "It is all right now. It's no longer a secret, but it *is* time he admitted it. We'll have time to catch up on everything. For now, go." She gave her a little push to start her on her way. "Bring food and water with you. Tell them they are welcome, but hurry. People are hungry."

New Woman turned back to help with the irrigation. Everyone was busy, digging, weeding, grinding corn, and cooking. So much had happened. She worked quickly and silently, thinking as she scooped handfuls of silt and mud out of the canals and piled them to the sides.

How much of her was still Four Cries? She knew she was no longer the little girl who cried because her father did not want her, but what would it be like to see him again?

"Will he come, Coyote?" she asked when they could speak.

"He'll have to now," he said. "He has no choice. It's either that or have his village starve."

"What will happen when he comes?" He left that question unanswered.

Crab, Otter, Coyote, and New Woman were waiting for them when they arrived. Young Momoy asked if New Woman wanted her to be there. "If you think it will help, I'll stand with you."

"No, Mother. I know you would do it. You were never afraid when something needed to be done, but there is no reason. It's time I faced him, alone." With Coyote, Crab, and Otter beside her, she was not really alone, but her mother knew what she meant.

He came into view. Her messengers, those who had come to Crab's village from Sa'aqtik'oy earlier, walked beside him to show him the way, but she could see they walked in silence. The people who walked after him were strangers to her now, but that did not matter. She could never turn away anyone who needed help.

Swordfish had grown thin, instead of muscular and lean. After two years without rain, everyone was thin. He must be close to forty years of age now. His face was gaunt, but his expression held the same stubbornness and pride. He was a man who was used to having his way.

Seahawk was the one who had argued with him. Seahawk remained in the valley. Swordfish had never known Crab or Otter. He had never really known her either. She stood between Crab and Otter. She saw him sizing her up, judging her power. He stopped before her.

"I thank you for your offer of food," he said. His voice was gruff. She realized with a start that she had forgotten how his voice sounded.

"I accept your generosity on behalf of my people, New Woman, but I do not know you."

"My messengers told you who I am." It was not a question.

"I never had a daughter." She tried to keep her face from showing any emotion.

"I accept peace. My people will share the work with Crab's people and Otter's people." He nodded to the two men who stood beside her. "But if there is to be a pacwot, to govern my village, Crab's, and Otter's while we live together until we can rebuild our homes, it must be me. I am the oldest and most experienced."

New Woman met his gaze. "That is not acceptable."

"Are you turning us away?"

He had found her weak spot. She could not do that. "We will discuss the situation after your people have been fed. I would not have them stand here and be hungry while we decide on terms."

The villagers of Sa'aqtik'oy who were close enough to hear murmured at this. She heard hoarse whispers of "She speaks wisely" and "Is she really his daughter?" Her old friend had done well. Swordfish turned to look at them sternly. The murmuring stopped.

"Follow me," she said, speaking to all. The villagers were brought to the valley in silence, except for the babies and small children, who cried from hunger. The food her messengers brought with them only made them hungry for more. They made her think of the Mojave children at the end of winter. How long had it been since they had eaten a decent meal?

Crab's villagers and the folk from Wene'mu watched as the new people were led to the ground before the ceremonial enclosure, the siliyik. There was not enough room for the hundreds of people. Some had to sit between the houses. It would be crowded here for sure.

"Bring food," New Woman said. "These people are hungry." Many hurried to do as she requested, coming through with baskets piled high with piki, the crisp bread of the Northerners. Water was brought also. Anyone with a thirst might dip into the water baskets.

After the Sa'aqtik'oyans had eaten, New Woman told her messengers to spread the word that they might be shown around. Crab, Otter, and all the Antap priests were invited to come into the siliyik. Swordfish's son, Little Fish, walked with his father.

The enclosure was built well of saplings and tule reeds. Part of it was covered, but not all. Old Momoy came inside. Whether or not she was still Antap, no one would dare to tell her no. Young Momoy walked with her.

New Woman noticed Swordfish looking at her mother. He recognized her and gave a momentary start, but he hid it well. Her mother's gaze did not flicker. There was only a hint of a smile on her lips.

Swordfish had his new alchuklash beside him, and his spokesman. Several Antap priests and priestesses stood with them as well.

Old Man came to stand beside New Woman. Perhaps Swordfish had been taken aback slightly by all that had happened. Certainly, seeing her mother had made him wince. He did not seem to realize who Old Man was. New Woman asked Old Man to speak for her.

He stood in front of them all. "New Woman is pacwot to all who come to this valley in peace," he began. "She is the one who brought the Easterners to join us and show us how to make food grow. Crab and Otter accept her." Both men muttered their agreement.

He faced Swordfish. "Can you not accept that?"

Swordfish spoke for himself. "I am oldest. A pacwot is a leader over leaders. Shall a young woman, barely out

209

of childhood, lead us all? Has she learned enough in her short years to govern over grown men? What of tradition?"

So it had come to that. Old Man consulted briefly with New Woman. Then he spoke again.

"You talk of tradition? What does tradition say about a father that runs into the women's birth lodge when a woman has just given birth? You did that almost fifteen years ago and this was the child." He turned New Woman to face all the people. "This is the child of the prophecy. I am Old Man from Sa'aqtik'oy."

There was a collective gasp on the part of all the Antap from Sa'aqtik'oy. Some of them had been there that day. Some of them remembered.

"Old Man?" "Is it really him?" The whispering stopped when Old Man held his staff before him. On it were a carved condor head and its feathers. They knew it was him.

"I don't believe you," Swordfish said. "I don't know you. I know nothing about a prophecy and I do not know this woman."

New Woman had come to the end of her patience now. In the face of all this, Swordfish insisted on maintaining his lie. Had he really come to believe it? She could see his own people were almost ready to turn on him.

She walked to where he stood with his son and spoke for herself at last. "Crab and Otter and all these priests say I have the right to govern here. If you think I need to do more to demonstrate that my rule is correct and in accordance with tradition in spite of my youth"—she turned to Little Fish and took his hand—"then I will marry your son."

"You can't," he said loudly.

"Why can't I?"

"You talk of tradition. To do that, you would break the oldest and strongest taboo in all of the Chumash lands." There was triumph in his voice. "You can't marry your own brother."

New Woman expelled a gentle breath, a soft sigh. She smiled at last. "Thank you, Father."

Swordfish realized too late what he said. She had outsmarted him. She had trapped him. His new al-chuklash took his arm. "I think you had better come away and compose yourself now," he told him. "Your son, Little Fish, is the new wot of Sa'aqtik'oy and its people. Accept it."

Swordfish looked once more at his daughter. She had tears on her face. He hung his head. Perhaps the prophecy had been true after all. He allowed himself to be led away.

Little Fish watched his father leave. Too much was happening too fast for him. He was wot now. He finally centered on New Woman. "Are you really my sister?" he asked.

"Yes, I am. I'm your older sister."

He did not know what to say. With a father like theirs, New Woman felt she understood why he lacked confidence. He would have to learn.

"You will be a good wot for your people," she encouraged him.

"I'll ask for advice from the priests," he said. "You'll help me?"

"Of course I will."

Crab, Otter, and Coyote came up to the two of them, smiling. "Brother," she said to him. "Cousin," she said to

Otter. "Friend," she said to Crab. "Dearest friend," she said to Coyote. "We will rebuild. We'll work together." No one will ever have to be hungry again."

A fine rain began. Sunflower began the cheering. Some of the others began to stamp their feet in rhythm. There would be new growth. The rain strengthened to a steady downpour. No one went inside. It felt wonderful. "It is truly the Mother's blessing today." The shouts were repeated over and over.

The dancing caught on. Soon the people of all three villages were dancing. Old Momoy came out to look at the dusty earth receiving the water. Young Momoy stood at her side with one arm over her foster mother's bony shoulder. "My daughter," the old woman murmured, "it's a day for being happy. Listen to my granddaughter. She's already making plans."

New Woman was speaking earnestly to Crab, Otter, and Little Fish about nets and tomols and acorns.

Old Momoy tapped her stick in rhythm to the dancing. Coyote sat on a rock in the rain and played a lively tune on his flute. He had to shake it out from time to time, but no one minded.

The Antap priests had Old Man in a welcoming circle on the dance floor within the enclosure, but open to the sky. Old Man sat and turned his face up to the rain, his eyes closed. His mouth was open to drink in the blessing of the earth, the sweet water from heaven, the giver of life. Then, he smiled.

AUTHOR'S NOTE

Chumash legend tells of a time long ago, "before the Flood," when animals were people. Not only animals, but certain plants, thunder, fog, the sun, and the moon were walking, talking people. The main deity of the Chumash was the spirit of the earth. Earth's spirit was sometimes called the Mother, but she was not personified in the same way.

Momoy is sometimes the name given to the plant datura. This plant has very special attributes. It was used by the Chumash and is still used by some southwestern people today to produce healing sleep and visions. Adolescents of long ago, at the time of their initiation into adulthood, were given a potion made of datura by the priests of the

Antap cult. The priests were able to guide the young person by interpreting his or her dream.

When Momoy was a person, she is said to have been a rich, old widow who lived in a valley of her own. In one story, she adopts a grandchild. She calls this child Tupnek, which means child in one of the dialects of Hokan, the Chumash language. Tupnek grows to be a great hunter who enjoys traveling with Coyote to have adventures.

Coyote himself is in many legends from both California and the Southwest. He has had so many things said about him that it is difficult to choose where to begin to describe him. He is said to be almost always hungry. He stuffs himself whenever he has the chance, but is always slender, perhaps because he usually goes a long time between meals. He enjoys music, singing, and dancing. He is sly, lazy, mischievous or wise, good or bad, depending on the story. He knows magic, but when his own magic is not enough to get him out of trouble, he calls on Momoy, who is able to help him from a distance.

In the old days, before the Antap priests initiated the adolescents, Coyote was Momoy's messenger. He went from village to village to bring them through their initiations. Sometimes in his travels he met Nunasis, supernatural beings, and got into trouble. He always got out again and was always ready for another adventure.

The Chumash occupied Southern California from Topanga Canyon and Malibu in the south to north of San Luis Obispo. All of the islands in the Santa Barbara Channel except Catalina were theirs. The woman who was left behind when her people were evacuated from San Nicholas Island to the Santa Barbara Mission (as told by Scott O'Dell in the *Island of the Blue Dolphins*) was a

Chumash girl, according to Chumash survivors I have spoken with.

They also told me another story they believe to be true. They say there was once a prediction made by an astrologer, before a child was born, that the child would grow to be a great chief, a pacwot, who would unite three villages under one government. This was in the days when relations between villages were not always peaceful. When the child was born, it was a girl. The astrologer was disgraced and made to leave his village. In time, however, the girl grew up and fulfilled the prophecy.

I have taken the story of this girl and combined it with the myths of Coyote and Momoy. Most myths have a basis in reality and this is how it might have happened.

The Northern People is my name for the ancient people known by the archaeologists as Anasazi. They lived in Chaco Canyon near where the borders of Arizona, Colorado, Utah, and New Mexico intersect. Anasazi is the name the Navaho give to the people of the cities there. The word means "our ancient enemies," which is why I could not call them by that name. At the time of the story, their culture and building were at the height of their growth, which places it in the middle of the tenth century by modern reckoning.

GLOSSARY

Alchuklash: astrologer, high priest, chief adviser to the wot

Atlatl: spear thrower

Antap: priest, plural or singular

Arroyo: a wash, or chasm made by heavy rains

Chupu: Mother Earth

Datura: hypnotic, dream-inducing plant cultivated by Momoy

Hokan: the language of the Chumash

Hutash: other name for Mother Earth

Keesh: house, round, made of saplings and reeds

Kiva: underground sleeping room for men or ceremonial room in the cities of the American southwest.

Nunasis: monster with supernatural powers

Pacwot: overchief
Pocheta: long-distance traders between the ancient cities of the "American" southwest and the Mexican cities
Pesbibata: tobacco, in North Country Hokan dialect
Siliyik: ceremonial enclosure
Temescal: Sweathouse—for purification and bathing
Tomol: a seaworthy craft, made by the Chumash of planks, tied together, sealed and made watertight with asphaltum
Tupnek: child, in the northern Hokan dialect
Wot: chief, leader

Tribes and their locations:

Anasazi: Chaco Canyon, near where New Mexico, Utah, Arizona, and Colorado meet
Basket Makers: another name of Anasazi
Cahuilla: near Pasadena
Chumash: Topanga Canyon to San Luis Obispo along coast of California
Hohokam: Southeastern New Mexico
Michumash: Santa Barbara Channel Islands
Mongollon: Southwestern New Mexico and northern Texas
Mojave: Desert people of the Mojave
Navaho: Called Marauders by Hohokam
Northeners: name of Anasazi in story
Olmec: Mexico
Tongva: San Fernando Valley
Toltec: Mexico
Topikar: Los Angeles